'There was nothing on earth or in hell that would have kept me from you!' Duncan Ross said slowly. 'From the day I saw you in London you have haunted me. I tried to thrust you from me but you would not go. When we met on the boat, I knew you would never leave me as long as I lived. You have become part of me. I do not want it! I resented you . . . I think at times I hated you, as you have hated me!'

'Oh, no, I never hated you! I thought you were harsh and unfriendly.'

'Because I had to fight to hide what I felt for you! Good heavens, when I thought of you tied to that weak stripling . . .'

Triona sprang to her feet. 'No! I am married to him!'

'Do you still love him, Triona?'

Ann Edgeworth was born in Dublin of Scottish-Irish parents and began her writing career by writing short stories and articles for women's magazines. She has lived abroad for many years, in places as far apart as the West Indies, Canada, West Germany, Sweden, France and Belgium.

Married, with three children, Ann Edgeworth lives in the West of England. *Lady of Flame* is her sixth Masquerade Historical Romance.

LADY OF
FLAME

ANN EDGEWORTH

MILLS & BOON LIMITED
15–16 BROOK'S MEWS
LONDON W1A 1DR

*First published in Great Britain 1985
by Mills & Boon Limited*

© Ann Edgeworth 1985

*Australian copyright 1985
Philippine copyright 1985
This edition 1985*

ISBN 0 263 74972 X

*Set in 10 on 11½ pt Linotron Times
04-0285–54,000*

*Photoset by Rowland Phototypesetting Ltd
Bury St Edmunds, Suffolk
Made and printed in Great Britain by
Cox & Wyman Ltd, Reading*

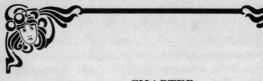

CHAPTER
ONE

THE LATE November sunlight pouring into the charming little morning-room struck gleams from well-polished silver and brass and turned the hair of a girl sitting in the window into an aureole of red-gold curls.

Triona Brooks, toying with her piece of tatting, looked around the room with a happy sigh. The new Wilton carpet gave the room an air of richness, and the plush curtains with draped pelmet added dignity to what had been a somewhat ordinary little parlour when she and Colin had bought the house. How lucky it was that dear Colin was so much appreciated by the London firm of importers who employed him that they had raised his salary, and she could now buy what she liked for the house and for herself. Dear Colin was always so generous. Money for pretty dresses and bonnets and for entertaining their new friends was always there.

Her thoughts were interrupted by the maid opening the door.

'Mrs Morton to see you, ma'am.'

'Aunt Jane!' Triona flung down her tatting and ran to the plump little woman in black cape and bonnet trimmed with jet, flinging her arms round her. 'How glad I am to see you! I am quite weary of my own company. Most of our friends are away, and Colin is so often out in the evenings at some stupid meeting or other.'

'And you have got your tatting in a sad tangle as usual,' her aunt said, smiling at her. 'How are you, child? And how is it poor Colin has to work so hard these days? You say he is often out in the evenings.'

'Oh, it is a perfect nuisance,' Triona said, tossing her curls. 'I should like to tell Mr Calder and Mr Oswald they have no right to expect a married man to spend his evenings at meetings or entertaining the firm's clients instead of being at home with his wife.'

'But they are a very fine firm, are they not? And dear Colin, you say, is doing well with them.' Mrs Morton looked around her. 'You have a most comfortable home, and more servants than I had when I first married.'

'Oh, Colin thinks we live in quite a poor way,' her niece said gaily. 'He insists we have a manservant, and we are to have a new carriage with two beautiful bay horses. But let me take your cape and bonnet. You will stay to lunch, Aunt Jane? I shall not let you go, although I do not know what kind of meal cook will provide. Colin is dissatisfied with her, and plans to hire a chef. We do a lot of entertaining, you know. It is delightful.'

Mrs Morton looked at her niece's lovely glowing face, and nodded.

'It is easy to see you are happy, my dear, and my heart rejoices for you. But—' She hesitated for a minute, then went on. 'But does Colin's income quite justify so much expensive entertaining? This is a large house and staff for a young married couple.'

'Ah, I know you think we are too young to live in such style,' Triona said smiling, as she took her aunt's cape and bonnet from her. 'You were, at first, perfectly against my marrying Colin, were you not?'

'Only because I considered sixteen to be so very young, and Colin only just twenty-one,' her aunt said.

'But we have been married one year now; we are quite an *old* married couple. Colin is doing so well with his firm that they have increased his salary several times, you know. We are thinking of taking a villa in Italy, somewhere by the sea, for a holiday in summer.' A faint frown touched Triona's forehead. 'Colin's father does not approve of the notion, I'm afraid, but then he approves of so little. He thinks Colin is extravagant, and I know he thinks me a poor housewife and too taken with pretty things and entertaining our friends.

'Canon Brooks has a stern nature, to be sure,' Mrs Morton said, seating herself on the sofa beside her niece. 'I sometimes wonder if he may have been a little too repressive as a father. But of course I must not think this, it is wrong of me to suggest a minister of the church could be . . .'

'Could be a bigoted, harsh and unkind father!' A spark of anger lit Triona's eyes, eyes as blue as a gentian. 'He is for ever scolding poor Colin, and Edward is little better! He has never been a kind brother to Colin, and the Canon has always favoured him.'

'Well, my dear, do not let us be uncharitable. Colin is very young, and his father's advice, though perhaps not welcome, may be of help to him one day.'

'I very much doubt it, but, as you say, dearest Aunt, do not let us discuss such a disagreeable subject. Now tell me what you have been doing, and if your rheumatism is better.'

She looked with affection at the aunt who had brought her up and given her all the loving care of a true mother. Triona's mother had died giving birth to her; her husband, wild with grief, had given the child into the care of his widowed sister-in-law and gone abroad, having arranged for a sum of money to be paid regularly for his daughter's keep and education. Some years later, news had come of his death from fever in Africa.

'I have little to tell you,' Mrs Morton said. 'You know how quiet my life is. My rheumatism, I am glad to say, has responded well to some new treatment. But tell me what you and Colin have been doing since we last met.'

'Oh we have been very gay, I assure you,' Triona told her happily. 'The Beaumonts gave a very fine ball and I wore my new blue gauze gown.'

She chatted on about parties, drives in the park, balls and the theatre. Suddenly she said, 'Colin and I have been so amused, Aunt. Some distant cousin of his father has left him an estate on a West Indian island called Ste-Martine. Now can you imagine the Canon living in a palm-thatched hut and growing coffee or cocoa or what ever they produce in those parts!' She began to laugh. 'I am sure he would try to reintroduce slavery! Colin says the island is a small one and quite unimportant. Of course the Canon will sell it.'

'Then I hope he will do so to his advantage . . .' her aunt was beginning, when the door opened.

The maid, looking flustered, said, 'Canon Brooks to see you, ma'am.' She was thrust aside as a tall, thin man in clerical clothes strode into the room.

'Triona, I must speak to you immediately on a matter of the greatest importance.' The Canon's eyes went to Mrs Morton, who rose hastily, saying, 'I shall leave you, Triona.'

'No, Aunt,' Triona caught her arm. 'Whatever Canon Brooks has to say to me shall be known to you. I insist you remain.' She turned to the Canon, her eyes suddenly wide and fearful. 'Colin . . . nothing has happened to him? An accident, or . . .'

'No accident,' her father-in-law said grimly. 'May I sit, please? I find myself greatly shaken by what has occurred.' He sank into a chair, letting his hat and stick fall to the floor.

'But what has happened?' Triona demanded. 'Oh, please, tell us, sir. What is this dreadful thing?'

The Canon took a moment to compose himself. His long, pale face, always stern, looked pinched and his eyes held barely suppressed anger. At last he said heavily, 'I had a visit this morning from Mr Calder, one of the partners in the firm which employs my son. He came to bring me the disastrous, almost unbelievable news that they have discovered that Colin for some time has been taking money—*stealing* money—from the firm that trusted him.' Two bright red spots had appeared on the Canon's cheeks and his eyes blazed as he stared at Triona.

Triona had gone very white. 'I refuse to believe it, sir.'

'Colin has admitted it to me. I sent for him and he revealed he has been gambling wildly, madly! That a son of mine . . .' The Canon drew a deep breath before going on in a voice that shook with rage. 'He has got into the company of a group of worthless and wealthy young scoundrels and began to "try his luck", as he expresses it. He *was* lucky, extremely lucky, at first.' His angry eyes swept the room and came to rest on Triona. 'You had your expensive gowns and bought new furniture and entertained your friends . . . He tells me he has ordered a carriage and pair!'

'The firm . . . They raised his salary . . .' Triona began, but he broke in harshly,

'They did not! And because he was not satisfactory in his work, Colin began to lose money. He mortgaged this house and furniture. All he has to say in extenuation of his criminal behaviour is that he means to repay the firm everything, given time.'

For a moment the room spun round Triona, then she felt her aunt's arm around her, steadying her.

'I—I cannot believe it! Colin is not a thief; he would never steal!'

'He has been proved a thief. My son has disgraced himself, and me! He is a criminal! What he has done is beyond forgiveness!'

Mrs Morton raised her head to look steadily into the Canon's distorted face.

'No man, sir, is beyond forgiveness. And if he repents . . .'

'Repent?' he spat the word at her. 'What good will that do? I disown him as my son! He has forfeited all claim to my affection. And you, girl,' he turned his burning eyes on Triona. 'You encouraged him in his wanton extravagance. But for you, he might have been content to live within his income. But you demanded finery, a luxurious life and . . .'

'I did not demand it!' Triona returned his angry gaze, her own eyes dark with shock and pain. 'I did not know he—he was gambling. He said he . . .' She bit her lip.

'He lied to you, no doubt, as he has lied to everyone.' The contempt in his voice made her wince. 'Well, he is ruined. There is but one course for him to take and I have shown it to him. Mr Calder will prosecute unless the money is paid back in full. I am prepared to pay what is owing out of my own pocket, on the condition that Colin leaves England. I shall make the estate on the West Indian island of Ste-Martine over to him, and he and you shall go there, immediately.' He got to his feet. 'I believe the estate has been neglected and I am prepared to pay Colin a living allowance until he is established. That is my ultimatum, and he will have to accept it. Good morning.'

The two women sat listening to his footsteps fading away and then the slam of the front door. The room was silent except for Triona's uneven breathing. Suddenly she buried her head on her aunt's shoulder and burst into wild tears.

'I—I can't believe it! It isn't true—it *can't* be true! Colin isn't a thief. There *was* a time when he seemed short of money, but then his firm paid him more . . . At least he said they did.' She raised her streaming eyes to her aunt's shocked and pitying face. 'Tell me it is a dreadful mistake, Aunt Jane!'

Her aunt bent to kiss her before saying gently, 'I am very much afraid it must be true, my dearest child, if Colin has admitted it to his father. It was terribly unwise of him to have gambled, but young men often do unwise things; Colin is very young and was influenced by wrong company. I truly believe he meant to return all the money he—he borrowed.' She sighed as she took out a handkerchief and wiped her niece's tears away. 'I *had* wondered sometimes how he could afford your style of living.'

Triona sat up, her eyes anguished. 'Aunt, he *has* lied to me. He was not working late or looking after clients in the evenings, as he told me. If I had known he was gambling I would have implored him to stop! I would have *made* him stop!'

'I know you would have tried, my child,' her aunt said sadly. 'But I fear there may be a vein of weakness in Colin's character that showed only when he got into wrong company. I most deeply regret what has happened and I regard the Canon's ultimatum to his son as both cruel and unchristian, but, my dearest child, you must face the facts bravely. If Colin does not agree to his father's ruling, he may be prosecuted and, I fear, found guilty, and there would be no hope of his finding further employment in this country. If Colin makes a success of this venture in the West Indies, it may well be that his father will forgive him and allow him to return home. You are both young . . .'

'And we must spend our lives on a run-down estate on a wretched little tropical island far from civilisation and all our friends! Heat, poisonous insects, tropical storms, black servants . . . We shall die there, Aunt Jane. I know we shall!'

'Hush, dear. You are naturally much upset, but you must calm yourself and think of Colin.'

'I cannot think of him without anger.'

'He is your husband, Triona,' the note of sternness in her aunt's voice made Triona look up swiftly. 'And you love him. It is your duty to help him now, not to condemn him. He needs you desperately, and do not forget that much of what he has done was to give you a more comfortable life.'

Triona was silent for a long time. She sat, her hand in her aunt's hand, staring into the fire as if seeing pictures of herself and Colin and what could lie ahead for them. At last she said wearily, 'I can't think clearly about things just now, I must have time. I still cannot believe this has happened.'

'No, it will take time.' Mrs Morton rose and went to the bell-pull. When the maid came, she ordered a glass of wine. 'You need it, my dear. Then you must rest.'

'No, no, I cannot rest. Stay with me, Aunt Jane.'

'Very well, until Colin comes. I think he will come soon, and then I will leave you. You must talk to him alone, and you must be merciful and understanding.' She sighed and murmured, half to herself, 'You are both so young . . .'

She watched Triona drink the wine, her heart sore at

the bleak despair on her niece's small, pointed face and the chill of fear in her gentian eyes.

Suddenly Triona sprang up, her eyes wide. 'It is Colin!'

Mrs Morton hastily donned cape and bonnet before kissing her niece tenderly and murmuring, 'Be a brave girl, my dearest, and try to help him.'

Triona stood still as marble, her hands clasped to her breast, trying to control the surge of emotion that threatened to engulf her. She heard quick steps that faltered before the door, and then stopped. A dizziness seized her and she caught at the back of a chair to steady herself as she waited. At last she saw the handle of the door turn slowly and the next moment her husband stood in the doorway, staring at her.

She was shocked at his appearance. The handsome, lively, debonair young gallant she had married was gone, and in his stead stood a broken youth, his stricken face unlovely with shock and despair. Her first thought was, *How changed he looks*, and she was instantly ashamed of it.

She steadied her voice with an effort. 'Your father has been here. Come and sit by me, Colin.'

He obeyed her, and buried his head in his hands with a groan that pierced her heart like a knife.

'Colin, my dearest, do not, I pray, give way,' she whispered, taking his hand in hers. 'It—it has been a shock to me, but indeed I know you never intended to *steal* the money and you had every intention of paying it back in full.'

He raised his head and she saw the tears on his twisted face.

'Oh, God bless you for that! Father, and Edward, would not believe me! Triona, I know it was wrong to gamble, but at first I was so lucky, I was able to buy things, things it was only right we should have. And I liked to see you in pretty dresses . . . and I knew how you longed for a smart carriage . . .'

'Oh, do not go on, Colin! I see how much was my fault!' She covered her face with trembling hands. 'I am so stupid about money, I never look at the bills when they come in. And I am a wretched housekeeper. But if only you had told me . . .'

'I didn't want you to know I had not received the rise in salary I should have got. I meant to give up gambling as soon as I had enough money to repay the firm. The fellows said it would be easy. They were a lively lot, amusing and a bit reckless, I suppose, and I enjoyed their company. Father condemns them, but they weren't bad fellows, Triona, only somewhat wild and careless.'

'And they persuaded you to join them in gambling,' she said miserably. 'Oh, Colin, *why*?'

'I've told you.' He sprang up and began to walk agitatedly about the room. 'We didn't have enough money to live as we *should* live. I hate penny-pinching. Father could have helped, had he wished, but of course my dear brother would never have allowed him to.'

Triona watched his restless pacing with unhappy eyes. Her aunt's words came back to her: '. . . sixteen is so very young, and Colin only just twenty-one.' She and Colin *had* been young, but they had been in love and impatient with their elders' cautious warnings and perfectly satisfied that they could manage their lives successfully. Too certain, perhaps. If she had been more experienced and had had more worldly knowledge, she might have had a better understanding of Colin. They had met one spring, fallen instantly in love, and had lived in a rosy dream of happiness. She realised for the first time how little they knew about each other. In the blissful year of marriage they had continued to live in their dream-world like children in a game of 'let's pretend'.

She straightened her slim shoulders, bracing herself for what she must say, knowing that for the moment she was the stronger.

'Colin, we must forget what has happened. It will not be easy at first, but we will try to put it behind us. Your father has told me of his offer to give you his estate on Ste-Martine in the West Indies . . .'

'Offer? He damned well ordered me to get out of England as soon as possible or I'd find myself in prison!' Colin swung round to face her, the misery and shame driven from his face by anger. 'I'll not go! To sweat myself to death on a godforsaken little island no one has ever heard of—*No!*'

'But what if you cannot get another position in this country? If we made the estate pay we could, in time, repay your father and be free to return.'

'How could I make a wretched cocoa estate pay when I know nothing of such things?'

'We could learn, Colin. Other people have.'

'And starve while learning.'

'Your father will give you a living allowance for a time,' she reminded him unhappily.

'Yes, a pittance!' Colin raised clenched fists in the air. 'How he, a professed Christian and minister of the church, can condemn me, his son, to a life where I shall surely rot! I tell you, Triona, it is hell on earth on these islands. Tropical diseases, stinking heat, endless work and trouble with the natives—and only outcasts washed up on its shores for me to mix with, the dregs of humanity who cannot fit into a civilised existence!'

'Colin, we do not *know*,' she pleaded. 'There may

be people like us with whom we can make friends. And we shall become used to the climate in time, I am sure.'

'I do not intend to try! I tell you, *I will not go*!' He swung round and rushed from the room, leaving Triona to stare after him with miserable eyes and cold fear in her heart. Whatever Colin might say, however much he might storm against his father's ruling, they had no alternative but to go out to Ste-Martine and make the best of it. It would be a humiliating and unhappy life at first, and Colin would hate it. From her despairing medley of emotions one chill little thought touched her before she could crush it: Colin had not once spoken of what life on Ste-Martine might mean to his wife.

During the next week Triona saw her husband only at breakfast and when he came, haggard and weary, to bed. She guessed he was desperately trying to find some way in which to avoid his father's orders and to obtain a position in another company, and she knew he had not succeeded by his morose silence and occasional angry outbursts.

She came back from a walk in the park one morning to find her brother-in-law awaiting her in the morning-room. Edward Brooks was taller and more heavily built than Colin and had none of his brother's charm of manner and handsome looks. He was sallow, like his father, and had the slightly pompous air of one who was well satisfied with himself. Triona had never liked him; when he rose to greet her, her manner was cool.

'I have come, my dear sister-in-law, to see if I may be of help to you in your plans.'

Her eyebrows rose. 'Plans?'

'Your arrangements for taking up a new life in the West Indies. There must be much to be seen to, and perhaps I may be of assistance. You know I am only too willing to help you and Colin in any way I can. In such tragic circumstances . . .'

'I do not consider them tragic,' she said as she drew off her gloves. 'Colin has not yet made up his mind to accept your father's offer of the estate.'

'Not accepted?' Edward's bland expression did not change, but an amused gleam came into his eyes as he studied her. 'But, my dear Triona, I'm afraid Colin has no choice. Calder will certainly prosecute if all the money is not repaid, and I greatly fear my father—you know how strict his principles are—will sacrifice so great a sum only if he knows Colin will go to the West Indies and make a life for himself and you out there. It is a rare chance for my brother to make a success of . . .'

'Of something about which he knows nothing, and in a strange country.' Triona's eyes sparkled dangerously. 'It is very easy for you to talk about it, Edward. You do not have to give up everything you cherish and enjoy and have to take on a life of harsh and perhaps dangerous living in a remote island among strangers.'

'If Colin had not behaved so . . .'

'I am aware how Colin has behaved,' she flung the words at him. 'And I do not condone it. But your father's judgment is too harsh.'

'He is of the opinion that Ste-Martine may be the making of Colin's character. He takes life too easily, my dear. He has never learned that, to succeed in getting what you want, you have to work for it.'

'Colin must make up his mind what he will do,' she said coldly, turning away. 'I shall, of course, abide by whatever he may decide.'

Edward picked up his hat and gloves. He gave a short laugh before saying, 'My dear Triona, Colin, as I said, has no choice. It is Ste-Martine or a prison sentence and disgrace for life. I bid you good morning.'

Triona stood twisting her hands nervously. If only Colin would tell her what he was going to do. The uncertainty was affecting her nerves badly. She did not sleep well and her appetite had gone, and frequent headaches plagued her. Only when she was with her aunt did she find any comfort.

Mrs Morton did not condemn Colin. She spoke of mistakes and weaknesses of youth, and the need Colin had of his wife's forgiveness and understanding at this time. 'I think perhaps a new life, even if it appears harsh and difficult now, may give Colin the chance of strengthening his character with the triumph of making a success of a new venture,' she said. 'It is a challenge, you know, and I am sure Colin will accept it in that light. It will be a great sadness to me to lose you, my dearest child, but I must be brave and bear the parting, since I know it is the best for Colin.'

'He has not yet said he will go to Ste-Martine.'

'I think he will tell you soon.'

Colin told her the next day. He looked weary and dispirited, and her heart sank at the hopelessness mingled with defiance of his words when he described his lack of success in finding work and his final accept-ance of his father's fiat. He refused to be comforted, and thrust aside all attempts to see the future in brighter colours.

'Since I must bury myself in such a hole, the sooner the better,' he burst out. 'It seems we are to take nothing from here. All is to be sold up. God knows what we shall find in Forest Estate—that is the name of the damned place!'

Triona bit her lip. 'Have you thought of trying to make the best of what is inevitable, Colin? I know life will be difficult . . .'

'Difficult? It will be unbearable!'

She suppressed the spurt of impatience his words aroused in her.

'If you are so determined to dwell on the darkest side . . .' she began.

He flung round to stare at her with furious eyes. 'There is no other side! Are you too stupid to realise my life is ruined? This is the end of me, I tell you!'

Suddenly her impatience melted in a small flame of anger. 'It is *not* the end, and your life is *not* ruined,' she said hotly, 'unless you make it so. To give way to despair will not help us. You must have courage, Colin.'

'How easy it is for you to say that! Have you once thought of what leaving my life here must mean to me?' he shouted. 'I leave all my friends, I leave my country and all I most value. I am dismissed as a criminal by a father who has no mercy, no pity . . .'

The sudden blaze in her eyes startled him into silence.

'Have you once thought of what this will mean to *me*, Colin?' she demanded. 'I realise now that I have been silly and extravagant, and perhaps I should have suspected something of what was happening and asked questions, but . . .'

'But of course it is all *my* fault,' his voice rose shrilly. 'Just because I tried to make life easier for you—for us! Hundreds of men take such chances as I did, but it was just my damned luck . . . If I could have had more time, all would be well, I tell you.'

'What has happened and whose fault it was is of no importance now,' she said wearily. 'That is over and we must forget it. It is the future that matters.'

'I have no future,' he muttered sullenly, turning away.

For a moment she was tempted to leave him to his sulky brooding. They were both at fault, but his was the greater part, and he knew it and the knowledge was bitter to him. He realised, as she did, that his father would never change his mind. He saw his son's behaviour as a crime for which he must be punished, and Edward would support him in that view.

Sudden remorse made her go to him. She slipped her hand in his and felt his fingers tighten on hers as she said gently, 'Colin, dear, we are young and healthy and not afraid of the future. We shall make a good thing of our life on Ste-Martine. The island may be very beautiful, and the climate pleasant once we get used to it. I shall help all I can. I shall learn to keep house there and manage the servants, and together we shall make a success of the estate. You will soon discover how such an estate must be managed; people will help us.'

He sighed heavily. 'I do not share your optimistic views, Triona. I see nothing but despair and frustration ahead of me. If I must go, I must, but life will be a living hell for me.' He put his hand to his brow. 'My head aches abominably. I am going to rest in my room.'

Left alone, she sat down to think. Since it was inevitable, they must leave as soon as possible, before Colin rebelled again. Colin's firm might become impatient if there were too long a delay and possibly start proceedings against him. She had no idea of how such things were done, but the threat was very real.

To sit and think of the past and the uncertain future did no good, and only increased her despondency. If she was to be of use to Colin, she must act.

She sprang up and called the maid to bring her jacket and bonnet and gloves. Outside the house she hailed a cab and told the man to drive to the offices of the Cunard Western Steamship Company, determined to make enquiries about sailings and length of voyage and what accommodation she might expect.

The office was busy and all the clerks occupied when

she arrived. She stood looking at the maps, and photographs of palm trees, seas with rolling breakers and smiling negroes. This was to be her life. Suddenly she was swept with fear. How could she survive being so far from everything she loved and had always known? To leave her beloved Aunt Jane, her friends, her charming and comfortable house and the gay, carefree life she was accustomed to in exchange for—what? A climate that would age her, perhaps failing health, hard work and isolation from congenial people?

Absorbed in unhappy thought, she did not notice the clerk beckon to her until a man standing at the counter touched her arm.

'Oh—Thank you, sir. I did not see he was free.' She moved to the counter and began to question the clerk.

'Ste-Martine, madam? I'm not quite sure where . . .' He produced a map and studied it. 'Ah, yes. There is no direct sailing to the island, I'm afraid. It is small and has little trade. You will have to go to St Lucia and from there take a local sailing.'

'Is St Lucia far from Ste-Martine?'

'Well, perhaps not *very* far,' the clerk said evasively. 'I don't know the precise time the journey would take.'

'Two days; more if there are high seas.'

Triona turned quickly to look at the man who had spoken, the man who had drawn her attention to the clerk. He was tall and broad-shouldered, deeply tanned, with thick dark hair and cool grey eyes. His features were good, a fine brow, thin nose and a well-cut mouth set in stern lines.

'Pray, what boats are there to take us to the island?' she asked him.

'Coastal steamers, and they are a poor lot, not over-reliable,' he said curtly.

'Do you know something of Ste-Martine, sir?' The

man's brusque manner displeased her, but perhaps she
might learn something from him.

For a moment he seemed reluctant to answer. 'Pretty
well. I live there.'

The clerk wrote out information for her; times of
sailing, types of accommodation and length of voyage,
and she put the paper in her purse. As she turned to go,
she saw the man who had spoken to her turn from the
counter with some papers in his hand. For a moment she
hesitated, but her desire for information was stronger
than her instinctive reluctance to approach him, and she
said quickly,

'Pardon me, sir, if I may trouble you to tell me a little
about the island of Ste-Martine?'

His dark brows rose. 'Ste-Martine? It is a small, hot,
green island with lazy natives, mosquitoes, cocoa and
some sugar-cane and forests.'

'Oh.' She heard the dismay in her voice and added
swiftly, 'Is there a town?'

He shrugged. 'Regina—recently renamed for our
Queen, although she will never have heard of it—is a
dusty little town with thieving shopkeepers. There is a
bank, hospital, police station and country club for Euro-
peans.' His cool eyes swept her briefly.

'Thank you for the information. My husband and I are
going out there.' A faint hope that he might tell her
something more reassuring made her add, 'We shall be
living on Forest Estate.'

He looked at her, small and slim, her vivid hair
escaping her modish bonnet; at her smart jacket, elabor-
ately draped skirt, expensive shoes and gloves, and a
grim smile touched his lips.

'Forest Estate? Old Haley's place?'

'Yes. Do you know it?' she asked eagerly, anxious for
any details he could give her.

His smile vanished. 'I know it. My own estate is next to it. Good morning, madam.' He raised his hat, bowed slightly, and strode away.

CHAPTER
TWO

LONDON WAS wrapped in a thin, grey, dismal fog that curled around the street lamps and crept down into house areas and set passers-by coughing and wiping their smarting eyes.

Triona stood in the window of the morning-room, looking out at the bleak scene. Bleakness was in the room, too, now it was stripped of its pretty flowered carpet, new curtains and the handsome furniture that she and Colin had bought with such joy only a short time ago. The house was quiet, as if, she thought sadly, it had died. Would something in Colin and her die too when they left the home that had been so pleasant and secure?

She turned slowly to her aunt, who was regarding her with unhappy and anxious eyes. Triona had grown thin in the weeks since the shock of Colin's disgrace. Her lovely blue eyes had dark shadows beneath them, and there were signs of strain in her face.

'Have you viewed your quarters on the *Scotia*, my dear?' Mrs Morton asked.

Triona shook her head. 'Colin is sure they will be cramped and old-fashioned. He says it is the last of Cunard's paddle-steamers and he is disappointed that we could not be on one of the new mail steamers. But even if our ship were the finest, he would find fault with it.' She sighed wearily. 'He is desperately unhappy, Aunt Jane, and I seem unable to help him.'

Her aunt joined her at the window. 'I think that is to be expected, my dear child. But, once you are on your way, I truly believe he will become interested in the voyage. And when you reach Ste-Martine, who knows but you may find it beautiful and the house capable of being made comfortable. Mr Haley—the Canon's cousin—was a bachelor and may not have lived in a very conventional way, perhaps, but I am sure you will set yourself to the task of making a home for yourself and Colin. And you will soon find friends, I expect.'

'Perhaps.' Triona brushed a red-gold lock of hair off her forehead and sighed again. 'There is an European Club in the town of Regina.'

'Now who told you that, dear?'

'A man who was in the shipping office.' For some reason Triona found herself reluctant to speak of the man. He had not been polite, and certainly not at all friendly. His appearance had not pleased her, and she considered his manner ungracious. He had shown no interest when she told him she was going out to Ste-Martine; in fact she had the impression the information did not please him. Why? Had he perhaps wanted to buy Forest Estate and add it to his own? Probably he had thought he could buy it cheaply, as few people would wish to live on such a remote little island.

'Did he tell you anything more about the island?' Mrs Morton asked.

'Only that it is hot, with mosquitoes and lazy natives. I didn't like him.' She forbore to mention that he would be their neighbour, choosing to ignore the idea since it displeased her.

The next few days were fully occupied with the final packing up, and buying such things as tropical clothes and medical supplies. Triona, on whose slender shoulders most of the work had fallen, sometimes found herself wishing she had ignored her instinctive reluctance to address the man in the steamship office and had asked his advice on what was most necessary for them to bring with them.

Colin, when she consulted him, shrugged his shoulders and said it made little difference what they took, as the servants would inevitably steal it or insects destroy it. He preserved a grim silence on everything to do with their journey, which Triona found hard to bear. She knew and sympathised with his feeling of humiliation and fear of the life he was going to, but she could have wished for a little more assistance in the unhappy business of preparing for their future life abroad.

Her aunt was her greatest help. The Canon and Edward had studiously kept away, and Triona had refused their half-hearted invitation to spend their last night in England with them, preferring sleep in the near-empty house to listening to the Canon's bitter comments and the unctuous utterances of Edward.

She had not spoken to Colin of the man in the steamship office. Any reference to their new home was painful to him, and she knew that as yet he had no interest in what they would find awaiting them.

'I shall be glad to be gone!' she exclaimed when the time came to bid Mrs Morton a sad farewell. 'Oh, I do not mean I am glad to leave you, dearest Aunt! I cannot bear to think I may never see you again! What shall I do without you?'

'You will be a loving and helpful wife and make a home for Colin and be his support until he becomes accustomed to his new life.'

'Be his support? What if *I* cannot accustom myself to a new life?'

Her aunt took her hand. 'Women are stronger than men in many ways, Triona; they have to be. Your task

will not be easy, and it may seem impossible to you at
times. But in your hands lies the success of your future.
And who knows but the estate will prosper, or Colin's
father relent, and you may return to England.' She
turned, as Colin came into the room. 'So all is settled,
Colin my dear, and you sail for the New World on
Monday.'

'Our transport is arranged,' he said in a brittle voice.
'But we do not travel to Botany Bay, only to green
stagnation on a stinking little island forgotten by the
civilised world.'

'All is packed and ready,' Triona said quickly, 'except
for the cases we shall need on the voyage. Your father
and brother say they cannot spare the time to see us
away.'

'Thank God for that!' Colin threw his hat on one of the
few chairs. 'Is there anything to eat, or must we starve?
Perhaps that is another plan of my respected father.'

'Aunt Jane has brought us a cooked chicken, and
there is fruit and bread.'

'And a bottle of wine,' Mrs Morton said, smiling.

Colin looked at her quickly before breaking into
laughter, the first laughter Triona had heard in many
days, and the sound lightened some of the burden on her
heart.

'Dear Aunt Jane! You are the world's most delightful
and understanding woman and I am a selfish beast! I
vent my misery on all of you because I am too weak to
keep it to myself. I am deeply sorry and ashamed.' He
slipped an arm around both women, smiling at them in
one of his startling changes of mood. 'Chicken and fruit
and wine! Bless you! I am going to enjoy the present and
let the future take care of itself. Isn't that what we should
do, Triona?'

'Oh *yes*,' she exclaimed, relief banishing the strain

from her face. 'I am quite certain the future *will* take care of itself and things will be much, much, better than we anticipate, Colin dearest.'

Colin's optimistic mood did not last, however. In the train taking them to Southampton he sat with folded arms and the shut-in look Triona had come to dread. She was still lost in sadness at leaving her beloved aunt, her friends and her gay and happy life, and for the moment she had no comfort to offer him. She sat looking out at the flying landscape, grey and bleak under driving rain, and thought wryly that perhaps it was as well she was leaving England when it was at its most unattractive.

In the bustle of going aboard the *Scotia* she had no time to think of what she was leaving or what she was going to. Colin gave impatient orders to the men handling their luggage and grumbled at the cabin that was to be theirs for the voyage, and she tried to pacify him by declaring that all was most neat and clean and they would do very well there.

He muttered something about needing a brandy, and left her. She went on deck to observe the other passengers straggle aboard amid shouting of orders, cries of farewell and shrieks of excited children. She was watching the scene with interest when her eye was suddenly caught by a tall figure she recognised shouldering his way through passengers and sailors for all the world as if they had not been there.

He strode up the gangway, his brown face remote and stern, and she turned away swiftly, not wishing him to notice her, but a few minutes later a voice behind her said,

'So we are to be fellow-passengers, Mrs Brooks,' and she turned to see the man she had met in the Cunard office.

She said, 'Yes, it would appear so, sir,' and meant to

say no more, but curiosity won the day. 'Pray, how did you know my name?'

'John Haley once told me he had left his estate to a relation in England of the name of Brooks,' he told her, easing a big leather bag off his shoulder as he spoke. 'It was my guess, and the right one, it seems.'

'The estate was left to my father-in-law, who has made it over to my husband.' She was not quite sure why she was telling him this. 'We are going out to live there. I think you said your estate was next to ours, Mr . . .'

'Duncan Ross,' he said reluctantly, and she wondered why he should dislike giving her his name when she could find it out easily enough on the boat and, most certainly, when she reached Ste-Martine. 'Have you and your husband any previous knowledge of managing a tropical plantation, Mrs Brooks?'

'No.' Her eyes were cold as they met his cynical grey ones. 'But we shall learn.'

A flicker of ironical amusement in his face whipped her quick temper into flame. She stiffened, her head high, as she said, 'We shall do very well. My husband is clever and hard-working. We shall not need any advice.'

He said, 'I have no intention of giving any,' and turned away, leaving her to stare after him and wishing she had not let her disastrously quick temper and the dislike she felt for him make her behave so curtly.

She did not like him, and it was most unfortunate that he lived near Forest Estate, but to be uncivil to your nearest neighbour was perhaps unwise. She did not want any advice from him, but it struck her now that Colin might be grateful for help if he should get into difficulties.

At last the bustle aboard ended, last farewells were said and the last handkerchief fluttered as the *Scotia* slid through Southampton Water on her long journey.

Triona and Colin stood at the rail, watching the fading rays of the winter sun pick out houses and church steeples above the busy shoreline before darkness fell. Colin's arm was around her, and he sighed and turned to look down at her.

'Well, sweetheart, we've said farewell to old England. God knows when we shall see her again. All is my fault. Oh, Triona, what a blind fool I was! I have brought you great unhappiness, I fear.'

'Hush, my darling.' She put her hand in his. 'Indeed you have brought me much happiness and joy always. You were foolish, yes, but who is not, sometimes? You took a dreadful risk, and lost. But we shall soon forget our old life in the excitement and interest of making a new one. You know, I am quite looking forward to doing some useful work, I have been disgracefully idle all my life.' She looked up at him and saw his face brighten. 'I believe we shall be happy on Ste-Martine.'

He bent and kissed her. 'God bless you. I could not go through all this if it were not for you.'

They stayed together, silent, their thoughts racing ahead. At last Triona stirred in his arms. 'It's getting cold. Let us go below. There are some mothers with children, and perhaps I can be of help to them.'

Her help was accepted gratefully. At supper she spoke to those nearest her and was soon on friendly terms with them, but Colin remained aloof, and after a few attempts at conversing with him, people left him alone. She went to her cabin early, tired out by the journey and emotion.

When Colin came, he awoke her, and she was pleased to see his gloomy mood had left him. 'There are some quite decent fellows on board,' he told her, balancing himself against the roll of the ship while he undressed. 'Most of them are getting off at Martinique or St Lucia.

But I've met a man called Ross who is heading for Ste-Martine and who—is it not strange?—owns Toco Estate, which adjoins ours. A curious coincidence.'

'Yes. I saw him in the steamship office, but of course I did not know who he was. Do you like him, Colin?'

He shrugged. 'He struck me as a rough fellow, brusque in manner and not over-social. I suppose he is a sample of what we shall find when we get to Ste-Martine. One of the officers told me Ross has a fine plantation and is doing well.' He gave a light laugh. 'Perhaps it is as well he lives near us, so that I can pick his brains. I've the devil of a lot to learn, you know. Ross made that pretty plain to me.'

'I think we can do very well without Mr Ross's help.' A bright spot of colour had come into Triona's cheeks as she looked up at her husband. 'I'm sure we shall find plenty of other neighbours to give us advice and perhaps help. There is a country club in the town of Regina.'

Colin looked surprised. 'How did you learn that?'

'I . . . someone mentioned it to me,' she said quickly.

'I didn't know you had met anyone who knew the island,' Colin said, kissing her before climbing into his berth. 'Who could it have been?'

'Oh, I believe Mr Ross did say a few words to me on the matter.' She was glad Colin could not see her flush of annoyance. 'I don't like him; he seems cold and un-friendly, and I trust we shall not see much of him in the future.'

'The officer who spoke of him said he doesn't mix much with people,' Colin remarked, yawning sleepily. 'So you need not trouble yourself.'

Triona had no intention of troubling herself about someone so unworthy of notice as Mr Duncan Ross. She fell asleep, wearied by the events of the day and undisturbed by the steady roll of the paddle-wheels.

She soon adapted herself to life aboard ship. Most of the passengers were pleasant, friendly people, with a few rough customers who kept to themselves. Colin seemed to have shaken off his gloom and despair and Triona's spirits continued to rise as they drew away from England.

After four days, they encountered some unpleasant rougher seas that distressed Colin and kept him and most of the passengers below decks. Triona, to her great relief, found she was a good sailor and enjoyed the peaceful isolation of the dining-room, except for the presence of Mr Duncan Ross, who, it appeared, was also a good sailor. He usually sat at the far end of the table and she could ignore him, but one evening the steward, no doubt with excellent intention, moved his place to opposite hers, so that she was obliged to acknowledge his presence, which she did in her coolest manner.

'We're having a touch of rough weather,' he remarked. 'But once past the Azores we'll calm down. I see you are an excellent sailor, Mrs Brooks.'

'Yes, but my husband is not, I fear,' she replied, and gave her attention to her supper.

The weather cleared, as he had said, when they passed the Azores. A pair of porpoises amused the passengers one day, and kittiwakes, a species of long-winged gull, followed the steamer for a while.

Triona grew restless. The restrictive life on board irked her and she longed to see land. Colin, too, complained of dullness and spent much of his time lying on his bunk reading.

The weather continued to improve, and the *Scotia* sailed into days of golden sunshine and gently rippling blue seas. Flying-fish fascinated everyone as they skimmed alongside the steamer, and sunsets became a glory of royal colours. Then, at last, a haze appeared on the horizon that was declared to be Martinique.

Triona and Colin watched the three peaks rise slowly from the sea.

'We shall dock at Fort-de-France,' he told her.

'We must go ashore,' she said. 'I long to feel land under my feet again.'

As they drifted into the harbour, engines silent and sails up, a swarm of small boats came to meet them with native women in bright turbans and gay cotton dresses who clambered aboard with their baskets of fruit, flowers and vegetables. The noise of their chatter filled the air. Triona bought some of the small bananas known as 'figs'. She found the heat, noise and brilliant colours bewildering but exciting.

The town was disappointing—drab, dusty and in parts ruined—and Triona was glad to return to the ship. Next morning she awoke to feel the rise and fall of the bows and knew they were easing out of the harbour. The next port of call would be St Lucia, from where they must take a local ship to Ste-Martine.

Some of the passengers had left the ship at Martinique, others were to leave at St Lucia, and there was a general feeling of excitement and unrest with the quick friendships fading as people became absorbed in their own plans.

'I wish to heaven old John Haley had had his estate on St Lucia,' Colin grumbled more than once. 'It sounds quite civilised compared with the wretched spot we're going to.'

'Oh, I expect we shall find it much more civilised than we expect,' Triona told him.

She was strolling on deck, the heat of the day having left as night approached, when Duncan Ross came up to her.

'We dock in St Lucia tomorrow,' he said abruptly.

'Have you plans for getting to Ste-Martine?'

'Well, not yet,' she answered. 'But Colin will find out about that when we reach the island. I believe you said something about local steamers?'

'I said they were a poor lot, and they are. I'm going over in old Jones's boat, the *Hummingbird*; it's the best of a bad lot. You had better arrange to come also.'

He made it sound so much like an order that she was tempted to tell him that she and Colin would make their own way to the island without his help, but she remembered in time how little they knew and much they might have to rely on such advice until they became accustomed to their new life. When she consulted Colin, she found him grateful for the information.

'Let us get to the estate as soon as we can,' he said impatiently. 'I'm wearied of this wretched journey. I want to find out just how things stand on the estate and what needs to be done there. You know, Triona, Ross could be very useful to us in many ways.'

'But, Colin, I would much rather you didn't . . .' She stopped. Colin would think her stupid to refuse any help that might be offered; he would not understand her feeling of hostility towards Duncan Ross. She was certain he would not be a pleasant neighbour, and she hoped fervently that they would see little of him.

They docked in Castries, St Lucia's capital, where there was the usual hubbub as native women came aboard. Triona said goodbye to her shipboard friends and followed Colin as he struggled through the dockside crowds. Suddenly she noticed that they were following the tall figure of Duncan Ross, and approaching a decrepit little shack with peeling paint and a notice-board advertising sailings aboard the *Hummingbird*. She waited outside while, she supposed, Colin was arranging for accommodation on the local steamer, and prayed there would be a sailing soon.

When Colin joined her, he said jubilantly, 'Well, I have managed that, my dear. Old Jones is a drunken old rascal, I would guess, but Ross says he knows these waters. There is a sailing tonight, and we can go aboard in two hours.'

CHAPTER
THREE

TRIONA'S FIRST glimpse of the *Hummingbird* gave her no reason to think the trip to Ste-Martine would be comfortable, or safe. The little coastal steamer looked old and dirty, its timbers were patched and all traces of paint had long since vanished, and her general air of being about to fall to pieces at any moment aroused the gravest apprehensions concerning what could happen if she encountered rough weather.

Colin, too, looked doubtful as they were rowed out, with their luggage, to where the ship lay rolling sluggishly, her timbers creaking, in the harbour.

'Ross says she's seaworthy,' he told Triona. 'She certainly does not look it, but if Ross says it is all right . . .'

'I suppose we shall have to accept Mr Ross's assurance,' Triona said. 'But I hope we need not meet him often when we are settled at Forest Estate, Colin. I don't like him—and I feel he resents our coming to the island.'

'Nonsense! Ross is not a social man and I can't say he has shown any signs of wishing to form a friendship, but there is no hostility towards us.'

Triona was silent. She considered Duncan Ross to be hostile in manner and intention. He had shown the barest courtesy to them. If his behaviour was a sample of what might be expected from other members of the colony, life was indeed going to be difficult and un-pleasant.

Ross had gone aboard earlier and was talking to Captain Jones, a weather-beaten, elderly man in dirty white trousers and ragged shirt around whom a faint and, Triona was to discover, permanent aroma of rum lingered. He advanced to meet them, displaying yellow, decaying teeth in a broad smile.

'Welcome aboard, ma'am. Glad to see you, sir. Make yourselves at home. We'll be going out 'bout sundown and should have a sweet little run and no trouble. Settling on Ste-Martine, ain't you?' His small bloodshot eyes held an ironic gleam as they inspected Colin's smart tropical suit, which his tailor had recommended, and Triona's pretty, frilled dress and gay little hat. 'Nice little island, you'll find it. Managing old Haley's place, ain't you?'

'It is my estate now,' Colin told him somewhat coldly.

'Is that so? Well I hope you and your good lady will make more of a success of it than poor old John did.' The captain chuckled. 'Left things much to themselves at the last, he did. I expect you'd like to see your cabin now. Follow me, please.'

Triona's suspicion that she would *not* like seeing the cabin was confirmed as she stared in dismay at the tiny, cramped room with two narrow bunks holding filthy covers, and the large brown cockroach leisurely crawling up one wall. The captain picked it up casually and threw it out of the porthole, remarking that the pesky creatures were everywhere.

'But they don't bite,' he assured Triona cheerfully. 'You'll get used to them, ma'am, if you're to make your home in the tropics. You'll find many worse.'

'Thank you,' she said hastily.' I don't think I wish to

hear about them just now, Captain. Please send me our smaller cases.'

As soon as he had gone she pulled off the bed-covers and flung them into a corner—and discovered another cockroach! She shrieked, 'Colin!' but he had backed out of the cabin in disgust.

'Something the matter?' Duncan Ross had to stoop to look in the door.

'Oh, take it away, please!' Triona begged him.

'What is it? Oh, cockroaches.' He came in and disposed of the insect as the captain had done. 'You'll find them in an old tub like this, they won't harm you.'

'But they are so horrid and so—so big,' she quavered. 'I shan't be able to sleep on that bunk!'

'I'll give you some powder.' He opened the leather case he carried. 'I take it when I travel. Sprinkle it around and it will keep the 'roaches away while you're here.' He gave her a tin, which she took eagerly.

'Oh, thank you, Mr Ross. I shall let you have it back.'

'Keep it,' he told her. 'I've plenty more. A meal will be served when we're a few miles out, but I've advised your husband to bring fruit and biscuits to eat in your cabin. The cuisine aboard the *Hummingbird* is not to be recommended but to those possessing strong stomachs.' He bowed and left the cabin.

'Yes, he did advise me,' Colin told her, 'and I'm grateful to him. I bought some things in the town.'

As the last rays of the sun on the harbour waters faded, the *Hummingbird* shivered and creaked protestingly as if unwilling to be woken from sleep, and set out, under sail, for the trip to Ste-Martine. She rolled badly although there was only a gentle swell in the rapidly darkening waters, and this, combined with the smells of cooking coming from the cook's galley, sent Colin to lie in his bunk, pale and unhappy.

Triona, once she had made him as comfortable as possible, went on deck, grateful for the cool evening breeze. Night was coming with startling swiftness and the lights of St Lucia were fading fast. Stars, bigger and brighter than eastern stars, spangled the purple sky above her and suddenly she was aware of beauty around her, the starlit sky and hiss of dark water breaking into silver foam along the old ship's sides and the wind, silken smooth against her face, brought an uplifting of her spirits and a wave of excitement. She had tied her hair in a scarf, but now she pulled it off and let her long red-gold curtain of hair swing about her shoulders, steadying herself aginst the roll of the ship as it surged through the darkness.

Something made her turn and she saw the figure of a man watching her. He was standing in shadow, his eyes on her as she stood under the light of a swinging lantern that lit the burning splendour of her hair.

'I'm sorry if I startled you.' Duncan Ross's voice was abrupt. 'I came up to get some fresh air.' He moved slowly forward, his eyes never leaving her. She had a sudden tingle of apprehension. He looked very tall and there was a curious expression on his lean face. 'Your hair—it is the colour of the immortelle that blazes in our forests. Flame of the Forest, people call it. I have never before seen a woman with hair like yours . . .'

She put her hands to her flying locks, feeling the blood rushing to her face. What right had he to spy on her and stare so boorishly with such intent eyes?

She brushed past him, murmuring, 'I found the cabin stifling. Good night, Mr Ross,' and hurried below, more than ever certain she did not like him.

The night was even more uncomfortable than she feared it would be. Colin became ill and moaned miserably. The heat was intense, and the bunks with their thin, lumpy mattresses made sleep impossible. Triona lay, letting her mind wander at will.

Her mood of happiness had gone as swiftly as it had come, and now memories crowded upon her: her aunt's loving face, her father-in-law's bitter condemnation of Colin, and Edward's smug condolences.

Abruptly, sweeping all else aside, she saw again a tall, broad-shouldered man with a dark, intense face and heard his words: 'Your hair . . . I have never before seen a woman with hair like yours . . .'

Morning came at last, and Colin slept. Triona dressed, ate some of the fruit and went on deck where Captain Jones was swearing at two negro deck-hands. He nodded to her.

'Trust you slept well, ma'am. Mr Ross's a gallant gentleman, ain't he? But any gentleman would give up his cabin for a lady as charming as yourself, ma'am, and that's a fact.' He grinned fatuously.

'Do you mean Mr Ross has given us his cabin?' she asked sharply.

'Ay, he has. Always has that cabin when he comes aboard. Truth is, ma'am, the other ain't as well set up, but he would have it, even though t'other cabin were engaged for him.'

Triona was silent, digesting the highly unpleasant fact that she must be grateful to a man she disliked. She told herself that of course any true gentleman would give up his cabin to a woman—but she could not help wishing it had been any other man than Duncan Ross. Even as she thought it, he came on deck.

'Just telling the little lady as how you'd let her and her husband have your cabin, sir,' the captain said affably, and was rewarded with a smothered oath and a look of intense irritation.

'I'd as soon you kept your mouth shut, Jones,' Ross

snapped. 'I didn't wish to sleep below. I am perfectly content to sleep on deck where at least I can breathe clean air.'

'Ay, it's stuffy enough below,' Captain Jones agreed, not a whit put out. 'You'll notice how sweetly we're going? We'll make good time to Ste-Martine, I reckon.'

'If this old wreck doesn't fall to pieces,' Ross growled ill-temperedly. 'And if you can keep sober enough to get us past the reefs.'

'Ah, you will have your little joke, sir,' Captain Jones said and shuffled away, whistling under his breath.

Triona braced herself to say, 'Mr Ross, I did not know we had taken your cabin.'

'Curse it, you weren't meant to know,' he replied grimly.

'I am grateful for your consideration,' she went on with an effort. 'My husband is not well; he barely slept at all.'

'And neither did you, I imagine. He is seasick? I've something that will help him. I'll go down to him.'

'Thank you.' Was she, Triona thought despairingly, for ever to be thanking this abrupt and unfriendly man? 'If indeed there is anything that would ease his discomfort . . .'

'There is,' he said, and left her.

When at last she returned to the cabin, she found Colin dressed and looking better. 'Ross gave me some beastly stuff that has set me right,' he told her. 'For goodness sake, let us get out of this hole and sit on deck.'

'But the sun is getting hot,' she protested.

'Ross says he will get the captain to rig up a bit of awning for us to sit under. I shall stifle if I stay down here any longer.'

Sitting under the shelter of the tattered piece of sailcoth and enjoying a refreshing if warm breeze,

Triona was able to relax, and Colin, though still pale and languid, looked happier than he had for some time. He spoke of Forest Estate with more enthusiasm than he had hitherto shown.

'Haley grew cocoa, but he grew a strain that, though of good quality, was not resistant to disease, and he had to replant with a hardier strain, which I believe he did about six years ago, but I gather the trees are not really profitable until they are older, so we shall have to wait awhile before we make our fortunes, Triona.'

'With the allowance your father gives us, we shall manage very well, I'm sure,' she said.

Colin's face darkened. 'I wish I was not forced to accept his charity! I want no favours from him!'

'But without his help we might find it difficult to live.'

'I doubt if he cares whether we live or die!' Colin exploded furiously. 'He could have paid what I owed and I would have repaid him in time. It is his damned pride that has made him send me to sweat myself to death on a run-down estate that may never pay its way.'

'We shall make it pay,' she said stoutly. 'Surely we can grow other things? Things we could sell? We shall see what the prospects are when we get there, Colin dear. Don't let us worry about it too much.'

'I believe there are two or three bungalows on the estate that Haley started to build, intending to rent them to government people, but he didn't finish them, the fool. We shall probably find his own house in pretty poor condition.'

'You have been talking to Mr Ross,' she said slowly. 'I wish you would avoid him, Colin. I know he has been helpful, but . . .'

'I hope he will continue to be helpful,' Colin interrupted. 'Can't you realise I shall need all the advice I can get? Ross grows sugar-cane and cocoa and does well out of it; he knows the island and its people and conditions there. I may make mistakes unless I can get advice on the best method of putting Forest Estate in order.'

'We shall meet other estate-owners,' she said stubbornly. 'They will be helpful, I am sure. We do not need Mr Ross to take us under his most unwilling wing.'

'Oh, you have taken a woman's antipathy to the man because he doesn't kiss your hand and pay you compliments,' Colin said sharply. 'Where are the papers we bought in St Lucia? I haven't read them yet.'

The old steamer surged steadily ahead, her timbers protesting when a deeper swell caused her to roll. Overhead, the sun blazed in a near-white sky and was reflected dazzlingly from the surrounding sea. An occasional scatter of flying-fish skimmed alongside the vessel, delighting Triona. The heat, blinding light and motion of the ship sent her into a half-dreaming state from which she did not awake until Colin announced that he felt hungry and would like some of the food he had bought on St Lucia.

The rest of the day passed peacefully. Colin dozed and Triona fetched her little writing-case and began a letter to her aunt.

Ross had come on deck but did not approach them, for which she was thankful. She felt even more uncomfortable in his presence since last night when he had seen her with her hair unbound and had spoken so strangely and, she considered, impertinently. She wished she had not removed her scarf; that she had remained in the stuffy little cabin; and that Duncan Ross lived anywhere but on the little island of Ste-Martine.

She and Colin managed to get some sleep that night, and awoke refreshed and with growing excitement as they neared the end of their long voyage. Triona searched anxiously for signs of land, and called to Colin when she saw a faint blur rising from the sea.

'That ain't your island, ma'am,' Captain Jones told her. 'That's St Vincent and the Grenadines, but I don't aim to call in this trip. We'll see Ste-Martine sometime tomorrow, 'cording to how the wind makes out.'

'Or how this old wreck lasts out,' Colin muttered. 'Thank God we'll be leaving her tomorrow.'

That night Colin told her the Captain had invited him to take a drink in his cabin with him and he would come to bed later. She lay in her narrow bunk, too excited to sleep, thinking of what lay before them tomorrow.

Duncan Ross would be with the captain and Colin, of course, and Colin would try to get all information he could from the man who was to be their nearest neighbour.

'I cannot blame him,' she thought. 'It is true, we do need advice. As long as *I* do not have to meet him, I don't mind too much. No doubt I shall find housekeeping strange at first, but I shall learn, I am *determined* to learn all I can so that we may make a success of our lives out here.'

The next day seemed to drag eternally. The provisions Colin had brought were finished and the mid-day meal of tough meat, over-cooked yams and tinned peaches provided by the ship's cook made Triona hope fervently they would not have to sample the evening meal.

It was late afternoon when Ross, standing at the rail, called to her. 'There she is, Mrs Brooks. We'll be running alongside and you will see where your estate lies.'

She joined him excitedly and saw a long line of brilliantly green trees and seas breaking over reefs.

'Coral Bay,' he told her. 'My place lies behind it. The little islet on the left is Frigate Island and there's good

fishing around it. We'll shortly be passing French Bay—
it's a wide bay without reefs—and then Forest Estate will
come in sight. The house is built on rising ground and
there are forests behind it that stretch to the centre spine
of hills. We go down to Sans Souci Point and turn to
make for Regina, port and capital. Carib Bay was once
the haunt of pirates, and the notorious Blackbeard is
supposed to have sheltered there more than once.'

Colin came to join them and together they watched
the green shoreline slide past. French Bay was a giant
bite taken out of the coastline and, once past it, Ross
pointed out the stretch of land rising from the shore with
a small jetty and told them it was their new home.
Behind, thickly wooded hills rose in waves to meet the
distant line of low mountains.

Triona's heart was beating quickly and, glancing at
Colin, she saw an answering excitement in his face. She
slipped her hand into his, whispering, 'There it is, Colin
dearest, our home! How beautiful it is! All those different shades of green—and that glorious flame-coloured
tree!'

'Flame of the Forest,' Ross's voice startled her, and
she sent him a swift glance as he stared across the water.
'The immortelle, that I mentioned to you. It is planted to
shade the young cocoa. As you remark, Mrs Brooks, it is
indeed a most glorious colour.'

She turned away abruptly. It was ridiculous, she told
herself, to think he meant anything by his words . . . and
yet there had been something in his voice . . . She caught
Colin's arm.

'Let us go below and see if we have packed everything,
Colin.'

He shook her hand off impatiently. 'You can go. I
want to watch how we round the point and enter the
harbour.'

Kneeling on her bunk, Triona watched while the ship swung around a narrow rocky point and continued along a shoreline edged with white sand and coconut palms. A canoe went past with negroes pulling in a fishing net. Palm-thatched huts, many built on stilts, appeared as they entered Carib Bay, on which the town of Regina was built. No longer able to contain her excitement, she went on deck to watch their approach to what seemed to her to be an untidy huddle of buildings marching up a hill that was crowned by a small white church.

She could see a wide street leading up from the docks, and, as they drew near, groups of coloured men and women sitting around or leaning against sheds, watching the steamer approach.

' 'Tisn't often they gets company,' Captain Jones explained to her. 'Mostly it's the craft as takes off the cocoa and sugar and fruits and such.'

'Do many people live in the town?'

'Not as you'd call the gentry, ma'am. Up the hill, near the church, is the fashionable part of Regina, and there's some good houses and a club and small hospital, the civilised part, you could call it.' He winked at her. 'Don't you judge the town by the docks and sheds and junk around 'em. The shops ain't too bad. The Commissioner has his place up in the hills behind the town. James Winkworth—the *Honourable* James Winkworth, Esquire! No doubt but you'll be meeting him and his lady.'

Small boats and canoes came out to meet them, and there was a bustle aboard as they slowly drew into the jetty. Then the chains were rattling through the hawse-hole and people were shouting greetings and Triona could feel the wave of heat coming from the land.

She and Colin bade the captain farewell and followed the men carrying their luggage. Colin looked around him in some uncertainty as the crowd milled around them.

'I suppose we can find some sort of transport to our estate? It will be dark soon.'

'I can take you and Mrs Brooks. It is on my way,' Duncan Ross said. He had shouldered his way through the crowd and was standing near them. 'Take what cases you need for the night, and I'll arrange for the rest to be brought up to the house tomorrow.'

'Thank you,' Triona responded faintly. Excitement, lack of sleep and the heat and noise around her was making her head swim. 'It is very kind of—of you . . .' she began, and heard Ross say sharply, 'Look out, she's going to faint!'

The next minute she felt herself being picked up and carried out of the crowd. For a moment everything blurred before her eyes. Then she heard Colin's anxious voice.

'Triona, are you ill, dearest?'

'No . . . No,' she murmured. 'It is only the heat . . .' She tried to move, but Ross's arms held her too strongly. She was lifted into a light carriage with an awning stretched overhead. A coloured groom stood by the two horses. Colin was beside her, his arm round her. 'Truly, I am quite recovered, Colin.' She sat up as her faintness passed away. 'I am sorry to have troubled you, Mr Ross.'

'It was no trouble,' he said coldly, and took the reins. It will soon be cooler.'

She and Colin were silent as Ross drove the carriage up the main street. Small shops, houses, a few gardens and vegetable patches lay on either side. Occasionally a better store, two-storeyed with a tin roof and jalousies, made surrounding shops look meaner. A pink building of some importance was, Ross told them, the police station and law court. Small brown and black children played in the dusty street, and women wearing bright cotton gowns and kerchiefs wound turban-fashion around their heads sat in doorways and stared curiously at the newcomers.

Strange smells, some less pleasant than others, came to them. A mule-cart laden with fruit and squawking hens in a wire cage passed them, and a tall, white-haired, swarthy man in a dirty white suit turned and waved to Ross, who returned his greeting.

'That is old Juan Geira,' he told Colin. 'He is Spanish and owns the biggest store.'

'He looks a pretty disreputable character,' Colin said indifferently.

They were now in the residential part of the small town. Pleasant wooden houses with corrugated tin roofs, verandas from which hung huge baskets of ferns, and cultivated gardens appeared. Tall palms added dignity to the scene and a blaze of purple bougainvillaea tumbling over a wall brought an exclamation of delight from Triona.

'Oh, how very beautiful! And that lovely tree with yellow blossoms!'

'That is a *poui*,' Ross told her.

They drove past the church and its neat churchyard, where two negroes were cutting the grass, and continued down a long dusty road lined with tall bamboos swaying gently in the breeze and giving a grateful shade.

Ross pointed out the Commissioner's residence. Triona said, 'I suppose we must call and write our names in the book there. Do they entertain much, Mr Ross?'

'I'm told so.' There was no mistaking the sudden coldness in his tone. 'I do not take part in the social scene, Mrs Brooks. I find my work fills my day very satisfactorily.'

'I see.' She thought it was more than possible that the inhabitants of the island had no particular wish to see much of Duncan Ross. He would be no ornament to society with his abrupt manner and arrogant bearing and rejection of any attempt towards friendliness.

Soon they had left the houses behind them and the road became rough, and dust rose to settle on clothes and damp hands and faces. Triona could feel her smart dress sticking to her hot skin and wished she had worn something cooler.

Her eyes began to tire of the brilliant green and gold and scarlet of trees and flowers. She felt dazed by the strangeness of the scene around her and longed to enter a cool house and wash and change her clothes.

'I suppose John Haley had servants, and they are expecting us?' Colin said suddenly, taking off his hat to wipe his perspiring forehead. 'I wrote to one Michael Jackson, whom I was told was managing the estate until I came out. No doubt he has seen to everything.'

A grim smile touched Ross's mouth. 'I've no doubt he would have arranged everything very comfortably—if I hadn't kicked him off the estate.'

'What did you say?' Colin turned to frown at Ross. 'You dismissed him? But he is in my employ! Just why should you take it upon yourself to dismiss him, may I ask?'

'Because, if I had not,' Ross said impatiently, 'he would have robbed you of the little Haley left you. That is why, Mr Brooks. Jackson was a rascal. He had been stealing from old Haley for years. When Haley died, Jackson had a splendid chance of getting his hands on everything and slipping away before you got here. I caught him removing stuff from the house, and told him I would set the police on him if he wasn't out of the island in two days. He went.'

'I see,' Colin murmured. 'I didn't realise . . . But why did John Haley employ such a man?'

Ross whipped the horses to a trot. 'Jackson was a heavy drinker and so, to be frank, was Haley. He'd have lived longer if Jackson hadn't kept him supplied with bad rum.'

Colin was silent. Triona saw the brooding, unhappy look on his face, and her heart contracted with pity. Colin was so vulnerable, so little able to withstand life's shocks and disappointments. But forced to face problems and difficulties he would, she was sure, grow in strength and wisdom. Until then, she must use her own strength. She turned to Ross, saying quietly and with dignity, 'We are grateful to you. We had, of course, no idea we could not trust the man. Shall we find any servants?'

'You will find cook, maid, washer-woman and house-boy. Here is your gate.'

It hung askew from rusty hinges, a wooden gate that had not been moved for years. The track leading into the grounds was pitted with holes and fringed with over-grown bushes. As they rounded a curve in the drive, Triona saw the house that was to be her and Colin's home, a single-storey wooden building. All paint had long since vanished from the warped boarding. A wooden shutter hung drunkenly from one window. A line of ragged washing hung near the house, and a tall negress wearing a patched cotton gown raised herself from a washtub to stare at them.

'Go and tell Melia Mr and Mrs Brooks have come,' Ross called to her. 'And get the boy to take the luggage.'

'Yas, sir, yas ma'am and mister!' The woman fled in the direction of several small palm-roofed shacks, call-ing shrilly.

Ross sprang down and, before she could prevent it,

had swung Triona to the ground. Colin was sitting perfectly still, staring at the house and untamed jungle of trees and shrubs and creepers around it, his face stony.

Triona went to him swiftly and touched his arm. 'Come, dear, let us go into the house.'

Colin did not move, but continued to stare. Suddenly he buried his head in his hands and groaned, 'My God! Oh my God!'

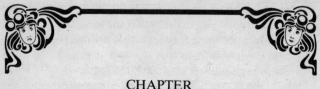

CHAPTER
FOUR

'QU'EST QUE DIT? Qu'est que dit?' the yellow and brown bird on the mango tree outside the bedroom window called with irritating monotony.

Triona stirred, yawned and opened her eyes. Sunlight came mistily through the mosquito curtain, touching the glory of her hair which lay unbound around her. She had long discarded nightcaps. Colin, sleeping beside her, had discarded all night-clothes in the heat which never ceased to plague him, and lay naked, breathing lightly, the worries of the day smoothed from his young face.

She slipped silently from under the net and went into the small room adjoining the bedroom where Amy, the negro maid, had left a bucket of water beside the enamel basin. After she had washed, she dressed in a loose white muslin robe and tied her hair back with a green ribbon. Leaving Colin to sleep, she went across the hall to the sitting-room, where breakfast awaited her.

Two months had passed since the day she and Colin had arrived at their new home. Colin still felt the heat, but she had become accustomed to it. They were coming into the dry season and were spared the abrupt thunderstorms and torrential rains of the wet season, weather which was responsible for the amazing lushness of the island.

She looked round her as she drank her coffee. They had employed a man to polish the neglected walls and

floors. Colin had wanted the walls to be painted, but
Triona was glad she had insisted on their being treated
with oil and polished, a process that brought out the fine
natural grain of the wood.

The outside shutters, which were let down only when
high winds or rain came, had been renewed, and the
outside of the house repainted. Such furniture as there
was could not be replaced yet, but Triona had brought
bright cotton and covered the sagging cushions and
made cloths for the scarred tables with their tell-tale
stains from wet glasses and spilt rum. A vase of purple
bougainvillaea blazed in one corner, and a few of her
precious pieces of china and glass, saved from the wreck
of their home, were arranged on shelves.

Colin had not been idle. After his first burst of despair, he had retreated into a brooding silence that had
chilled Triona's heart. Then he seemed suddenly to face
up to a life that was foreign and hateful to him and had
set about discovering in what state the cocoa trees were,
and what must be done to harvest the crop, and how to
manage the negro workers.

A few neighbours had called and had been friendly
and helpful. Triona had learned how to order food,
manage Melia the cook and Amy, a mulatto, and Han-
nah, the big washer-woman, who at first had tried to
cheat her but, on discovering this to be impossible, had
developed a healthy respect for her new mistress.

They had not seen Duncan Ross since the day they
had arrived on the island. Triona noticed that his name
was not often mentioned among her neighbours and,
when it was, there was a noticeable reserve. It was the
old Spanish storekeeper, Juan Geira, who told her that
Ross had arrived on the island four years ago and bought
Toco Estate.

'A very fine estate he gets,' he assured her. 'It was well

planted and cared for. And Señor Ross learns quick, like that!' He snapped his bony fingers. 'He makes much money, I think. He also grows cocoa and some tobacco. It is not wise to put all the eggs on one basket, no?'

The Forest Estate cocoa was young and would not yield full crops for some years, but at least John Haley had planted the *Forastero* strain which was strong and reasonably resistant to disease. There was, of course, always the chance of the dreaded witchbroom or the cocoa-beetle that attacked the roots of the trees.

Duncan Ross did not, Triona discovered, belong to the country club, and she did not meet him at any of the few social functions. He stayed, silent, self-sufficient and hard-working, on his estate, asking for, and giving, no signs of friendship.

There was a banana plantation behind Forest House, and at Triona's suggestion the hands were cut and taken to the town market in the mule-cart.

'And we have pawpaws and oranges and limes,' she told Colin. 'We must sell them.'

He resisted at first, saying they would fetch little money and it was a waste of the house-boy's time. Wisely, she did not press the matter. Colin was still prey to fluctuating moods and easily became irritable. She busied herself with improving the house and making plans for a vegetable garden.

She was aware of the curiosity their arrival on the island had caused, and had learned to parry too-inquisitive questions, letting it be known that the estate had been left to Colin's family. Since the English climate did not suit Colin, she explained, they had decided to make a home in a warmer part of the world.

She was in Juan Geira's shop one morning. Sam, the young negro boy who fulfilled the roles of house-boy, groom and general handyman, having driven her into the town in the shabby little one-horse buggy, had just finished paying for her purchases when a tall figure blocked the doorway and she looked up to see Duncan Ross. He bade her good morning.

'Ah, Señor Ross,' Juan Geira called. 'You come for your corn, no? How are your chickens doing?'

'Well, I trust. I'm growing my own corn, so you need no longer supply me.' He turned to Triona. 'Do you keep chickens, Mrs Brooks? They and their eggs are useful additions to the menu.'

'I shall think about it.' She looked away, aware of his eyes on her, and illogically pleased that she was wearing one of her charming light-coloured cambric dresses that displayed her slim figure so well. But annoyance came swiftly on the heels of her pleasure. Why should she feel gratified because she was well dressed, when Duncan Ross's admiration, or lack of it, meant nothing to her? It was feminine vanity, she told herself, and she would do well to curb it.

'Juan will find you some fowls,' he told her, 'and can supply you with corn to feed them until you grow your own.'

'Oh-oh!' The man rolled his eyes dramatically. 'How do I make money if no one buys my corn?'

'By cheating customers who don't watch you like a hawk,' Ross said unkindly.

'Indeed it is you who are like a hawk, señor.' Juan Geira turned to Triona. 'Is he not like a hawk, señora? A fierce and cruel hawk who knows no will but his own?'

A hawk? Yes, she thought, casting him a swift glance from under the shade of her hat. The lean dark face, hawk-like nose, stern mouth and arrogant bearing were those of a man who would acknowledge no will but his own. What Ross wanted, he would take.

As she turned to the door, his voice arrested her. 'I

haven't seen your husband, but tell him from me it would be wise to think of having other crops as well as cocoa. Arrowroot is good, and grows well here. You have some excellent fruit. From here we export fruit and vegetables to St Vincent and other islands, and you will find a market there.'

'I am already arranging to send fruit down when the boat calls,' she told him. 'I shall tell my husband what you have said.'

'Do you want a gardener?' he asked abruptly. 'I know a young coolie—they're the best gardeners—whom I can recommend.'

She hesitated, remembering Colin's rejection of her suggestion that they should grow vegetables and fruit and send them to market. Suddenly she made up her mind. 'Very well, Mr Ross. Send me the man. What is his name?'

'Ram Takoor. He's a Hindu and completely reliable.'

She thanked him and left the store. As she came out into the blinding white sunlight, she saw a smart little carriage with a woman in it, and recognised Mrs Grantley, an Irishwoman who had managed a small estate alone since her husband died. She was a warm, friendly, gossipy woman with a cheerful and humorous view of life, and Triona had liked her immediately on meeting her.

'There now,' Mrs Grantley called out. 'I thought that was your buggy, Mrs Brooks. Have you done shopping? Then come back with me and we'll have a chat in the house. Tell your boy to collect your parcels and call for you in two hours.'

Triona agreed eagerly. It would be a pleasant change from the monotony of her life to visit another house and talk to another woman.

'Wasn't that Duncan Ross I saw going into Juan's?'

Mrs Grantley asked as they drove up the hill at a spanking pace. 'I believe he must have been on the same boat with you coming out.'

'Yes, he was,' Triona murmured.

'Ah, I expect you found him a hard nut to crack,' Mrs Grantley said, nodding her head and setting the scarlet poppies adorning her hat dancing. 'The poor man has a cold manner with women.'

'I certainly found him somewhat unfriendly. At least—' a faint sense of guilt made her hesitate. 'Well, he *was* helpful to us in some ways. He gave up his cabin to us in that dreadful little boat. And he has given my husband some advice, I believe, about the estate.'

'He'll do well to take it,' Mrs Grantley said firmly. 'Duncan is no fool. He has the most prosperous estate on the island. He treats his workers well and pays them well, and works himself to death.'

'He appears somewhat of a recluse.'

'He's no use for the social life and maybe he's wise in his ways, seeing how things are with him.' Mrs Grantley looked thoughtfully at the passing scenery and said no more until they pulled up before a long white house with green jalousies and creeper-covered veranda.

Triona followed her into the pleasant coolness of the house. A maid brought iced orange-juice and sweet biscuits, and Mrs Grantley settled herself for a chat.

'Now, tell me how you are managing. Are your servants behaving themselves? Send them off if they aren't; there are plenty more. They'll respect you if you're firm and stand no nonsense. Did you live a gay life in London? What were the fashions when you left? Did you ever catch sight of the Empress Eugénie? I'm told she was a great beauty.'

Triona did her best to satisfy her hostess and spoke of balls and drives in the parks, concerts and the ballet, and

Mr William Morris, whose aesthetic movement was becoming all the rage.

Mrs Grantley listened eagerly. 'Ah, it must have been a fine life, my dear, and how you must miss it. Aren't you dreadfully homesick at times?'

'Why, I—I . . .' To her horror, Triona felt swift tears gather and spill over in her eyes. 'Oh dear! Yes, I *am*, Mrs Grantley! Oh please forgive my silliness . . .'

'Why now, there's nothing to forgive, my dear. Wasn't I the greatest trial to my husband, weeping and keening all day for the Wicklow Hills till I drove him mad? It will pass, my dear. Keep busy and you'll not have time to brood.'

'Th-thank you, dear Mrs Grantley.' As Triona fumbled for her handkerchief, she heard the maid say something, and a second later Mrs Grantley exclaimed,

'Duncan! It isn't often you pay me a visit.'

Triona, aware of her tear-wet face, sprang to her feet, dismay sweeping over her. At the same moment she found Mrs Grantley beside her.

'Poor Mrs Brooks's eyes aren't yet used to our sunshine. She's having great trouble with them and the way they water after she's been in the town with all its dust and everything.' She led Triona aside and, taking her handkerchief, wiped away the tell-tale tears, bestowing a kindly wink on her as she did so. 'I was just telling her I had the same trouble when I first came here. You must bathe your eyes in salt and water; that will strengthen them.'

'Thank you, I shall,' Triona murmured gratefully. Ross was standing in the doorway with some letters in his hand.

'Some mail came in unexpectedly today,' he said. 'I've brought yours, Norah, and Mrs Brooks's. I saw she had gone with you.'

'Oh, letters from home!' Triona exclaimed joyfully, and was threatened by a renewal of tears. She saw that two were from her aunt, and one for Colin from his father.

'Will you have a rum punch, Duncan?' Mrs Grantley asked hospitably, but he shook his head.

'No, thank you, I must get back.' He nodded brusquely and strode out of the room, greatly to Triona's relief.

'That man works too hard and too long,' Mrs Grantley remarked, reseating herself and motioning Triona to do the same. 'He drives himself cruelly, and he's had enough of cruelty in his life.'

Triona looked up, her attention caught by the words. 'Has Mr Ross suffered, then?'

Mrs Grantley played with the rings on her plump fingers and for a moment was silent. Then she said, 'There is a tragedy in his life that would have ruined another man. But Duncan is strong; he has had to be, to withstand his life out here.' She looked up, her eyes suddenly serious as she said, 'Mrs Brooks, you'll hear many things about Duncan; folk here have little to do but remember and gossip. Don't listen to all you'll hear. I know the man better than most, and I'll never believe . . .' She looked at the maid in the doorway. 'What is it, Minny?'

'Mistress Brooks's carriage done arrive, ma'am.'

Triona rose, thanked her friend and left. As she was driven back along the dusty road she wondered what tragedy clouded the life of Duncan Ross and if it was their memory of the past that made people avoid him so obviously. Some unhappy event might account for his withdrawing from society, but not for his abrupt manner and uncouth behaviour. If indeed he had suffered, she must be sorry for him—but she would never be able to like him.

Colin was sprawled in a chair on the veranda when she reached the house. 'Where have you been? It is nearly lunch-time,' he complained.

She told him of her visit, and gave him his letter, and went to remove her hat and wash her hot face and hands. Colin was so often irritable these days. The heat continued to distress him, and the bareness of the house and the lack of familiar comforts made him restless. He was looking pale, and was languid in the mornings, often rising late and with no appetite for his breakfast. He was spending more time at the country club, and she was glad he found the company of other men there with whom he could talk.

'Must we for ever eat fish and rice?' he asked as they sat down to lunch.

'The fish is always fresh,' she said. 'And we have rice because you do not like yam or sweet potatoes. Melia cooks fish pleasantly, I think, in coconut milk. Colin, I think we should buy some hens. Melia will look after them.'

'And steal the eggs, no doubt.'

Colin, she realised with an inward sigh, was in a difficult mood, and she decided it was not the moment to tell him she was about to hire a coolie gardener. Already she and Colin had had small quarrels over various matters, which distressed her. She glanced across the table at him as he picked moodily at his food, and thought, with sinking heart, how much he had changed in the two months on the island.

Have I changed too? she thought uneasily. *I don't think I am as good-tempered or patient. I don't always agree with Colin now. I even find myself criticising him . . .*

His letter brought him no pleasure, apparently. After

reading it, he crumpled it angrily and threw it away, making no comment upon its contents.

'So you've been visiting Mrs Grantley,' he remarked abruptly. 'You had better take care—she is a gossip.'

'Who told you that?'

'Oh Frank . . . or somebody,' he said carelessly, but the name had caught her attention.

'Was it Frank Cunha? I didn't know you knew him. Did you meet him at the club?'

'No.' He pushed his plate away. 'He doesn't trouble himself with the club. He's a business-man with too many interests to spend his time exchanging gossip and drinking rum punches at the club.'

Triona said no more, but she was uneasy. Frank Cunha was a half-caste Portuguese, and one of his biggest interests was the rum shop in Regina. She wondered where Colin had met him, but she was too wise to ask, and risk an outburst of complaints that she resented his making his own friends and spending time with them.

Colin, she knew, was doing his best to adjust to his new life as a planter. He was busy, with Big Jim, the negro overseer who had worked for John Haley, in planning for the harvesting of the cocoa crop that was about to begin, and the engaging of trained men and women needed to pick the pods and extract the beans, the latter work being known as 'breaking cocoa'.

Triona had walked among the trees, watching the pods turn red as they ripened. Shade for the young bushes was provided by trees, among them the immortelle.

The coolie gardener, Ram Takoor, made his appearance. He was a small, thin, brown young man wearing a flat straw hat, white cotton shirt and loose cotton trousers. Triona liked his manner and engaged him and arranged for him to occupy one of the little palm-thatched huts in the servants' compound. She told Colin that night about their new gardener, and was relieved to find he approved.

The cocoa-cropping began and at first Colin was interested in the work. The ripe fruit was gathered by a special tool fixed to the end of a bamboo pole. The pickers were followed by men and women who gathered the scattered pods in baskets and emptied them into a heap. Later, the pods were cut open most dextrously, and the beans were removed. This work was done mostly by women and children, who sang as they worked.

From there, Colin told her, the beans would be put in the fermenting boxes to dry by exposure to the sun and wind and eventually bagged for marketing. Triona found the work deeply interesting, but Colin soon tired and left the overseeing of it to Big Jim.

The weather became cooler, and Triona found much pleasure in taking an occasional drive to see something of the island. The vivid greens of the forests stretching up to the central hills, and the bright colour of the flowers—hibiscus, bougainvillaea, plumbago and lilies—were a joy to her eyes. Great ferns grew in the forests and creepers hung from tree to tree. Tiny green parrots chattered in the tree-tops.

'Oh, yes, I suppose it is all quite pretty,' Elsie Clayton, the young and lively wife of a government official, remarked to her. 'But there are snakes there, you know, not the harmless ones we see around the house, but dreadfully horrid things like the fer-de-lance and the coral snake. It quite frightens me to think of them! I am so glad we shall be returning to England this year.'

The Honourable James Winkworth held a garden-party in the grounds of the handsome residence above the town. When the invitation came, Colin at first refused to accept it, saying he had no taste for dressing up and meeting people he did not wish to know. But Triona, with a delightful pale green poplin gown and rose-trimmed hat in mind, managed to persuade him that it would be considered an affront to the Crown to stay away.

The occasion was a pleasant one. The pretty dresses and gay hats and frilled parasols reminded Triona of Henley and summer strolls in the parks at home. The Honourable James was something of a disappointment, being a small sandy-haired and self-important man with a fussy manner and restless disposition. His wife was tall, thin and plain, and looked with disapproving eyes and pursed mouth at the butterfly ladies flitting about the well-kept lawns.

'She is quite *dreadfully* prim and proper,' Elsie Clayton whispered mischievously to Triona. 'She would like us all to dress in brown, as she does. Her dinner-parties are disastrously dull; she talks about the Dear Queen . . . Indeed, I quite believe she thinks *she* is queen here and in charge of all our morals!'

Mrs Grantley bore down upon them, splendidly arrayed in violet silk, her hat swathed in pink silk net and velvet pansies.

'My dear Mrs Brooks, you're a vision in that gown! I'm the cooler just for looking at you. And that lovely hair of yours . . . Archie,' she turned to the young man at her side, 'Isn't Mrs Brooks a picture? Have you been introduced? Mrs Brooks, this creature is Mr Archie Hallam. He is just out from England and is surprised to find we don't dress in palm-leaves and live on coconuts and wild pig.'

'Oh, come now, Mrs Grantley,' the young man protested, smiling at Triona. 'We do know something about the West Indies, you know. The ladies' costumes here would grace any royal garden-party at home.'

'Well, I doubt if mine would,' Mrs Grantley said candidly. 'Her Majesty isn't one for cheerful colours, I'm told. Now Alicia Winkworth would suit her splendidly. Isn't that bonnet of hers the greatest tragedy?'

Triona liked Archie Hallam. He was a fresh-faced, good-looking and cheerful young man of the type she had known so well in London, and she was glad to have him by her side while she wandered about the grounds admiring the flowers and flowering trees. He told her he was to be attached to the Winkworth household as assistant to the Honourable James. His conversation amused her, and she was laughing at some of his comments on the passengers on his ship when she caught sight of Colin staring at her angrily. She slipped away with a murmured excuse.

'What is it, Colin?' she asked anxiously. 'Are you tired? They are about to serve tea . . .'

'I do not wish any tea,' he said abruptly. 'If you find amusement in exchanging vapid remarks with these people, *I* do not. Who is that cocky stripling who has been ogling you, pray?'

'Oh, Colin, he hasn't. He is Mr Hallam, and he is most pleasant.' She felt her pleasure in the afternoon fade as she saw the deepening ill-temper on Colin's face. 'If you are not enjoying it, perhaps we had better leave,' she said dispiritedly. 'Ask a servant to call for our carriage.'

He did so, and they drove back in a silence that brought a chill to her heart. A weariness crept over her, draining away her happiness and excitement in wearing her pretty dress and meeting her friends.

'A waste of an afternoon,' Colin said sourly when they were in the house. 'I shall never go again.'

'I don't suppose we shall be asked,' Triona said, pulling the pins out of her hat.

'That would give me the greatest pleasure.' He dropped into a chair.

She looked at him as he lay, his hands hanging limply over the arms of the chair and his legs stretched out, and at the frown he so often wore now and the sullen line of his mouth. The face of a self-pitying, spoiled child—and suddenly a flame of anger burned her.

'*You* found no pleasure,' she said fiercely, her eyes blazing. '*I* enjoyed it—but you did not think of that, Colin! Must you always be thinking of yourself? This life is hard for you, but it is hard for me, too. I did not wish to leave England and all I love! We came here because of you . . .' She broke off abruptly. She had never reproached Colin for his unhappy weakness, and she would not do it now. Already her swift flare of anger was dying.

But it was too late. Colin had risen and was looking at her, his face shocked and furious. His voice shook as he said, 'So that is what you think of me, is it? I am charmed to know you blame me for everything and consider me a selfish beast!'

'Colin, I don't. Please . . .'

'It is true! You have grown to despise me. You amuse yourself with your friends and never think of the miseries I have to endure!' He snatched up his hat and turned to go. 'At least I do not have to stay and listen to your spiteful ragings. I too have friends and I shall go to them!'

He rushed from the house and she heard him calling to Sam to saddle the horse and bring it round. She stood, her hands gripped together, sick with apprehension. What was happening to her and Colin and to their marriage?

My wretched temper, she thought in anguish. *Oh, why cannot I control it better? He is right, he does have miseries I do not have to endure. I must be patient, more understanding and loving.*

She waited, watching the shadows darken and night envelop the land, hearing the nightly chorus of croaking frogs and cicadas start up. Outside, the leaves of the mango tree rustled gently. A soft murmuring, some-times breaking into song, came faintly from the servants' quarters. The sound of a trotting horse made her spring up and run to the window, but the rider passed the gate and the sound faded.

When the little clock her aunt had given her struck midnight, she went to her room and lay, her eyes wide and fearful, waiting. Where was Colin? Had the horse shied at a shadow and thrown him? Was he even now lying unconscious by the side of the road, hurt—perhaps dangerously? Fear twisted her heart.

Suddenly she sat up, every nerve alert. What was that sound? Wheels stopping outside the house, voices—a knock on the front door!

She sprang from bed and snatched at her dressing-gown. As she opened her door and ran into the hall, she heard Duncan Ross's voice.

'Hold him up, Ram . . .'

She had left the lamp burning. By its light, as she opened the door, she saw Ross and the young Hindu gardener carrying a limp figure . . . *Colin*!

'What has happened?' she gasped, icy fear gripping her. 'Is he—is he . . .'

'Please stand aside,' Ross's voice was completely without expression. 'In here, Ram, put him on the bed. It's all right, Mrs Brooks, he isn't dead.'

They had taken Colin into the bedroom and laid him on the bed. Ram slipped noiselessly away into the darkness. Triona clutched Ross's arm.

'He is injured! Is it bad? Will he . . .'

'He will recover.' The abrupt harshness of his voice made her shrink back, startled and shocked. 'Give him black coffee, lots of it, when he awakens.'

'Coffee?' She looked at him, bewildered.

'Your husband is quite magnificently drunk, Mrs Brooks.'

Relief . . . horror . . . anger . . . swept her as she stared at him.

'I do not believe it!'

But already the smell of rum was apparent. Colin muttered something thickly and rolled over, burying his head in the pillow.

'Where did you find him?' she whispered through dry lips.

'That doesn't matter. I got Ram to give me a hand, and you need not fear he will talk. Ram will always be loyal to you, you can count on that. Now, will you be all right? It will be better not to rouse the servants. I suggest you try and get some sleep . . . in the other bedroom.'

She nodded, unable to speak. She must thank him—but the words refused to come. Suddenly she became aware of how she must appear, her muslin wrapper thrown hastily around her, her bare feet and her hair flowing over her shoulders like a living flame in the lamp's soft light.

He was looking at her, and his look made her tremble as colour flooded into her face. He did not move. His hawk's eyes seemed to burn her, and her heart began to race uncontrollably. Suddenly he strode forward and caught her by her shoulders, his fingers gripping her soft flesh cruelly.

'My God! What made a woman like you marry such as

he? A weakling who leaves you alone while he drinks with the scum of the town! You are beautiful . . .'

'Let me go! How dare you speak to me in such a way!' She put her hands against his chest, feeling the hard strength of him, and pushed him away. He released her and stood looking down at her with something in his face that made her tremble. 'Go!' she whispered. 'You are behaving unforgivably!'

A curious smile touched his lips. 'I do not ask or expect your forgiveness. Although, if I had not picked up your husband tonight . . .' Before she could move, he caught her hand and kissed the palm. 'I'll take that as my reward,' he said harshly, and swung on his heel. A moment later she heard his horse plunge under the lash of a whip and the carriage wheels spin as they turned. Then all sound died but for the whisper of the wind and the cicadas' monotonous clamour.

Triona stood as if turned to stone. Her hand seemed to burn where his lips had rested. She shut her eyes, trying to crush down the hot surge of emotion that frightened her.

'Triona!' The hoarse whisper reached her and she shivered, then turned.

'I shall make you some coffee, Colin.'

CHAPTER
FIVE

COLIN'S REMORSE was painful to witness, but slowly his abasement merged into condemnation of Triona's behaviour.

'If you had not spoken so unfeelingly, so cruelly, to me it would not have happened,' he complained, and she knew he was already placing all blame on her. 'Your abuse drove me from the house. You have never shown such spiteful temper before, Triona.'

'I am sorry,' she said wearily. They were sitting on the veranda in the late afternoon, listening to the distant singing of the cocoa-pickers, and Colin was staring out of the window with red-rimmed eyes that studiously avoided hers.

She watched a little gecko, a house lizard, run up the wall and across the ceiling, trying to banish the images that so persistently haunted her.

Colin, his clothes stained and creased, sprawled on the bed. Ross looking at her unbound hair and thin wrapper with a sudden leap in his eyes that had burned her. Despite her resolution to forget, she felt her blood stir as she remembered that look and felt again his kiss on her hand.

She wrenched her thoughts back to Colin. How many people knew of last night's events? Instinct told her Ross would say nothing, and he had said Ram Takoor could be trusted to keep silent. What would have happened if

Ross had not found Colin and brought him home? She owed him gratitude for that, no matter how insolent his behaviour had been.

A sudden restlessness drove her out of the house. Ram was gathering up his hoe and cutlass. He bowed when he saw her, his brown face devoid of all expression. 'Master's horse come back safe, Mistress Brooks,' he said.

'Oh—I'm glad to know that; I had been wondering about it.' She turned away, embarrassed and ashamed. Yet why should she feel Colin's lapse so acutely when many of the men on the island drank, and often to excess. Colin had gone to town to forget for a little while the memory of her outburst and a life he hated.

When she returned to the veranda, Colin was moodily drinking the black coffee Melia had brought him.

'What would you like for dinner, Colin?' Triona tried to make her voice cheerful. 'Melia has cooked a nice young chicken.'

'I do not feel like eating anything . . . Oh well, perhaps a little chicken.' Abruptly he caught her hand and looked up at her. 'Triona, you aren't angry with me? You don't hate me?'

'Oh no, Colin dear,' she smiled at him. 'We shall forget about it.'

'It was everything.' His voice held a weariness that went to her heart. 'That stupid garden-party and the young fool who was making you laugh. You don't laugh often now, Triona. Are you unhappy?'

'Of course not,' she assured him swiftly. 'I find life here interesting and I have made some good friends. Truly, I am happy.'

He sighed. 'I wish I felt as you do. And my respected father does not make things better by writing me sermons.'

'His letter did not please you?'

'I threw it away.'

When they were preparing for bed, he startled her by saying with a laugh, 'I was not the only customer at Frank's last night, Ross was there also—rather luckily for me.'

'He was drinking?'

'Why else does anyone go to Frank's?' Colin crawled in under the mosquito net. 'He has a much stronger head than I. Probably he finds a welcome that he gets nowhere else on the island.'

'Do you know why that is?'

He shrugged. 'I gather there is something in his past that makes people avoid him somewhat.' He looked up. 'I have just remembered something, Triona. When we first met, he asked us to visit Toco Estate next Sunday.'

'But of course we shall not go,' she said quickly. 'You know I do not like him.'

'Nonsense, Triona. You are perfectly childish about the man,' Colin said, yawning. 'His past history is nothing to us, and *I* do not dislike him. Anyway, I have to be grateful to him for last night.'

She was silent, knowing that if she persisted in her refusal to go with him to Toco there would be another distressing quarrel. She dare not risk telling Colin of Ross's behaviour, knowing how unpredictable his temper had become. He had been jealous of poor Archie Hallam's attentions at the garden-party, which had meant nothing. Of course Ross's behaviour might also have meant nothing.

He had been drinking, she thought as she slipped into bed, and he is a rough man unused to the society of women. He may not have realised how insulting his manner was to me . . . And it is true that I must be grateful for his rescuing Colin.

What would have happened if Ross had not been there? Would Frank Cunha have sent a message asking her to come and take her husband home? If Colin had remained in the sleazy little rum shop until morning, all the town would have known of it.

She must forget last night. Possibly it had already slipped from Ross's memory. To refuse to meet him would bring further embarrassment, and trouble with Colin.

After breakfast next morning the maid, Amy, came to Triona with her face streaked with tears as she told of an accident to her mother and the message that she had sent for her daughter to come and look after her. 'She break she leg bad,' Amy sobbed. 'She old and need help. She don't have no man and I is the onliest child she have. I must go to she.'

'Of course you must go,' Triona told her kindly. Amy was lazy and her work left much to be desired, but she was a cheerful, honest girl. 'I shall pay you your wages and you can go at once.'

When she told Colin, he grumbled. 'Probably it is all lies. She is too lazy to work. You must get another girl, and a better one this time. By the way, I met Ross this morning and told him we would be visiting Toco on Sunday.'

Triona sighed. 'Very well, since you wish it. But I shall not enjoy it.'

The next morning, she was admiring some of the tubs of flowering plants on the veranda, when something made her look up. A girl stood watching her. She was tall and slim and obviously of mixed blood. Her skin was pale gold with a silky sheen, and her features delicate and slightly oriental, and her wide, slanting eyes were beautiful. She wore a simple cotton gown that did not completely conceal the graceful lines of her young body.

'Who are you?' Triona asked in some surprise. 'What do you want?'

'My name is Lara, Mistress Brooks.' Her voice was soft and husky. 'I hear you want a house-girl to work for you.'

'How did you hear?'

She spread her slim hands. 'I hear.'

'How fast news travels. Yes, I shall be needing another maid. Where do you come from, Lara, and who has employed you?'

'My home is Petertown, ma'am.' She gestured to the range of hills. 'I work for Mistress Smith, but she dead and she husband go to Barbados. I work good and know how to wait at table. Mr Smith give me this.' She pulled a folded paper from her pocket and gave it to Triona.

It was an excellent recommendation. Mr Smith wrote of the devoted service to his invalid wife, and the girl's honesty and capacity for hard work. Triona handed the note back.

'Very well, Lara, you can come and work for me for a month, and if you are satisfactory, I shall keep you.'

The girl curtsyed. 'Thank you, ma'am. I come tomorrow.'

Triona watched her walk away, admiring the girl's graceful carriage and thinking how lucky it was that she need search no further for a maid. When Melia was told of the new arrival, she shook her turbaned head.

'I don't never hear of she, ma'am. Petertown lie way over on west coast. Amy say she sad to leave you, she say you is a nice nice lady.'

Triona laughed, and pushed back a strand of red-gold hair that had fallen across her forehead. Suddenly the cook said,

'Peoples is saying your hair is most beautiful, ma'am,

just like the Flame of the Forest. They is always calling
you Lady of Flame.'

'That is very nice of them, Melia. Now, what can we
have for dinner? Mr Brooks is tired of fish.'

Triona awoke early on Sunday morning. For a moment she lay blinking sleepily and wondering at her
curious mixture of dread and excitement. Then she
remembered.

She slipped from bed and went to the wardrobe. The
day promised to be fine. The quick breeze shaking the
leaves of the palms promised relief from unpleasant
heat. Her white Swiss muslin with rose ribbon trimming?
Or the lilac cotton with a slight train? She caught sight of
the leaf-green gown she had worn at the garden-party
and remembered that Mrs Grantley had admired it, and
so had Archie Hallam. It would not appear too elaborate
a costume if she wore a plain straw hat with it.

When they were at breakfast, she looked across the
table at Colin sprinkling lime juice on his slice of pawpaw. His cheerful expression told her he was looking
forward to the visit to Toco Estate.

He said, 'Ross has asked us for lunch, and we are to be
there early to see the fields and sugar-mill before it gets
too hot.' He pushed his cup across for more coffee. 'By
the way, is that the new maid in the kitchen? What is her
name?'

'Lara. People called Smith employed her and gave her
an excellent reference.'

'She is an improvement on the other girl. Can you be
ready by eleven o'clock?'

Triona said she could. Today there would not be time
to attend service in the little white church in the town.
She had persuaded Colin to go once with her; at other
times she went alone. She had met and liked the Rev.
Ernest Fisher and his wife, a friendly, simple couple who

had made her welcome to the community.

When she appeared in the green dress and wide white hat, Colin's eyebrows rose.

'Do you plan to overwhelm Ross as you overwhelmed young Hallam?' he asked with a smile.

'I doubt if anything less than a typhoon could overwhelm Duncan Ross,' she said composedly. 'My dress is cool, and since there will be few garden-parties to attend, I may as well wear it before insects attack it.'

Toco House stood on ground that sloped sharply down to Coral Bay. It was a wide, one-storey building, larger and better constructed than Forest House. The winding avenue was lined with well-trimmed bushes and tall palms and ended in a gravelled sweep around which ran a low stone wall with scarlet and purple bougain-villaea rioting over it.

As they drove up, Ross came to meet them. His white shirt was open, showing his strong brown neck. Once again, Triona was conscious of the force of his personality which could dominate a situation, and she looked away swiftly, not wishing to be made aware of how his personality diminished Colin's. He took them into the house, where coffee was served in a long room that seemed bare to Triona but had beauty in the polished cedarwood walls and the wide windows looking out over the sea.

She exclaimed, 'Oh, how lovely!' and went to the window and stood looking at the rocky fall of land ending in white sand and emerald sea. A tiny fishing-boat dipped and rose as it crossed the bay, which was sheltered by an arm of coral reef against which waves rolled to burst into a spray of silver spume.

'Are you interested in seeing the sugar-cane and how it is worked, Mrs Brooks?' Ross asked.

'Yes,' Colin answered for her. 'And so am I. Perhaps

you can tell us something about it? How it grows and how it is harvested.'

'The cane was brought to the West Indies in the sixteenth century,' Ross told them. 'It does well here, because of the good rainfall we have. It grows all the year round and crops ripen every month.'

'It sounds an easy crop,' Colin remarked.

'We have problems. The cane can be attacked by a variety of pests, mostly beetles that bore into the stems, and there is the wireworm. But froghoppers are the worst.'

When they had finished their coffee, he ordered the house-boy to bring the small American-type buggy to the door and drove them out to the cane-fields, where the great feathery tufts of flowers rippled in the breeze. Planted so thickly that no wind could pass through the stout, much-jointed stems, the cane grew like a giant grass up to nearly ten feet high.

Ross explained that the cane was usually dug up and replanted after a few years. Crops were harvested ten months after planting and when the flowers appeared. Then the stems were cut at the base by men wielding cutlasses, the leaves taken off, and the cane loaded on ox-carts and taken to the primitive little sugar-mill where it was cut into short lengths and forced through rollers to extract the juice.

He took them to see the sugar-mill and the giant black iron pans in which the juice was boiled until it formed a thick syrup which cooled into crystals of coarse brown sugar.

In spite of herself, Triona was caught up in the interest of what Ross showed them. She asked about the workers.

'Most of them are Indian,' he told her as he drove them back to the house. 'The negro doesn't like working cane. Indians were imported and have proved good and reliable workers. I trust you are satisfied with Ram Takoor, Mrs Brooks?'

She looked away, murmuring that she found the Indian a good worker. All at once she was overcome with the memory of the night Ram had helped Ross to bring Colin home, and she remained silent and constrained for the rest of the drive.

Luncheon was excellent: king-fish followed by chicken pilau, pigeon peas and flowery yams, and rum fritters.

'It's remarkable how well the native cooks manage on their coal-pots,' Colin observed when they were having coffee in the sitting room. 'Melia doesn't do at all badly. We have acquired a new girl; she looks half-Chinese and comes from the west coast where she worked for some people called Smith.'

Ross looked up quickly. 'What's the girl's name?' he asked Triona.

'Lara, I don't know her other name.'

She had the impression he was going to say more, but instead he turned to Colin to ask about the cocoa crop.

She drifted into daydreams as she sat by the window, her eyes on the changing colours of the bay below. Coconut palms growing at grotesque angles fringed the beach, the mid-day sun burnishing their ragged fronds. Near the window a jewel-bright hummingbird hovered over a spray of plumbago. The island was beautiful, she thought, more beautiful than she had expected. Perhaps in time she would come to love it and forget the memories of England that still had the power to bring pain.

Suddenly she heard Ross say, 'I expect Mrs Brooks would like to see the rest of the house.' He had risen and was standing before her.

Her first impulse was to refuse, but Colin laughed and said, 'Oh, she'll enjoy that, I know. Women delight in looking over houses. Is that a new copy of *The Times*?' He picked up the paper and began reading it.

Ross led the way and Triona followed unwillingly, uneasy at the idea of being alone with him and wishing she had pleaded weariness as an excuse to remain with Colin.

The house was plainly furnished, but what there was, was good. It caught the sea winds and was refreshingly cool. Ross took her into his office, where books and papers lay on desk and chairs. A large water-colour of an immortelle tree in all its blazing glory hung on one wall.

Except for a few appreciative remarks, Triona had been silent, trying to make up her mind. Now she took a swift breath and said, 'Mr Ross, I wish to express gratitude for your help to my husband.' Her tone was formal and she did not look at him.

There was a silence in which she could hear the keskidees asking their endless question: 'Qu'est que dit?'

'You have nothing to thank me for.' The harshness of his voice startled her. 'But you must not let your husband make a friend of Frank Cunha. No good will come of it.'

She stiffened indignantly, resenting the implication of his words. 'I do not tell my husband what he may and may not do, Mr Ross,' she said sharply. 'I am afraid I must ask you to keep your opinions of Colin and what I should do to yourself. We do not need or seek your advice. I am sorry to have to say this . . .'

He came close, and she saw his eyes were no longer coolly impersonal but like blazing steel.

'You are not sorry! You have wished to say something

like this to me from the start. You hate me! Admit it—or are you afraid to?'

'Afraid?' She returned his burning gaze, her own eyes dark with anger. 'I am not in the least afraid of you! Yes, I do dislike you and I greatly resent your manner towards me. You have behaved like a—a boor. I hope I may not have to meet you again!'

He gripped her arm, pulling her to him. Fear rose in her and a strange, trembling excitement.

'You are right, it is better we do not meet. Why in heaven's name did you have to come out here? A woman of flame . . .' His voice sank to a whisper. 'A flame that can burn a man.'

She wrenched herself free, her heart beating so wildly that for a moment the room swam around her. He caught her as she swayed.

'Triona, forgive me, I should not have . . .'

'Don't touch me!' She thrust him away with trembling hands. 'And do not call me Triona! Order our carriage, I shall leave at once!'

He stepped back, his eyes narrowing and his face grim.

'You may put down my behaviour to the fact that I haven't seen a beautiful woman for a long time. Living as an outcast does not bring out the best in a man. I shall keep out of your way, you may be sure of that. But, I repeat, do not let your husband get involved with Cunha and his friends . . . and get rid of your half-Chinese maid.'

She walked from the room, her head high and her lips compressed. Not for worlds would she let him suspect the sensations she experienced at the touch of his hand on her arm. Outwardly calm but inwardly deeply shaken, she told Colin she was affected by the heat and wished to return immediately to Forest House.

At his protestations, Ross broke in curtly to say that their carriage was ready and that probably Mrs Brooks had overtaxed her strength that morning.

When they got home, Colin burst out irritably, 'What is the matter with you, Triona? You were perfectly all right. I wanted to ask Ross . . .'

'You must do without his advice, Colin,' she broke in sharply. 'Mr Ross can never be a friend. I find him ill-mannered and quite unacceptable.'

'*You* find him unacceptable?' Colin's young face was flushed as he stared at her. 'Well, *I* do not find him so! And I refuse to be told I cannot accept any man's friendship! *I* am master here, please remember. I am going to the club. Do not wait dinner for me; I shall dine there.'

He flung out of the room and she heard him call to Sam to bring his horse.

She sank into a chair, swept by feelings of anger and fear. Ross's unforgivable behaviour . . . Colin's burst of temper . . .

The sound of wheels brought her to her feet. A visitor was the last thing she wished for, but it was too late to escape. Lara opened the door, to announce, 'Mistress Clayton to see you, ma'am.'

The next minute Elsie Clayton, in ruffled pink cambric and flowery hat, was crying, 'Dear Mrs Brooks, I was visiting nearby and thought I must drop in to see you!'

'How kind. Won't you sit down?' Triona pulled herself together with an effort. 'Would you like some refreshment—tea or a fruit drink?'

'Tea would be perfectly *marvellous*.' Elsie discarded her parasol and dropped into a chair with a sigh of satisfacton. 'Isn't it strange that we should enjoy hot tea so much in this climate? I suppose it reminds us of

England.' She stared around her. 'How nice you have made this room. I'm afraid I haven't done much to our bungalow, since we shall be returning shortly to England.'

Lara came in with the tray of tea and withdrew with her graceful swaying walk. Elsie's eyes followed her.

'What a pretty little creature. Quite oriental, isn't she? I'm so glad I've found you in. Someone told me they had seen your carriage drive into Toco Estate this morning.'

'Yes. My husband is anxious to know about various crops, and wished to consult Mr Ross.'

'And insisted you went with him.' Elsie accepted a cup of tea and sighed. 'Husbands are *so* inconsiderate, aren't they? My husband has invited the vicar and his dowdy little wife to dine with us next week, and I know I shall be quite horribly bored. It must be very awkward having Mr Ross living so near. I mean, so difficult to avoid him.'

'As everyone else does. Why do they, Mrs Clayton?'

Elsie put down her cup to stare. 'My dear Mrs Brooks, don't you know?'

Something cold touched Triona. She said quickly, 'We have not been here long. I have not heard anything.'

Elsie's face brightened with the tattler's delight in discovering a new outlet for gossip. 'Then you don't know he was hounded out of Trinidad?'

Triona caught her breath sharply. '*Hounded?* Why?'

'Oh, it was perfectly *dreadful*! Duncan Ross had to leave Trinidad because he was suspected of murdering his young and beautiful wife!'

CHAPTER
SIX

SHOCK HELD Triona silent for some minutes.

'It cannot be true!'

'Oh, it was quite a dreadful scandal. His wife was found stabbed to death on the veranda of the house. She had been about to run away with another man and had left a letter for Ross. Of course it was *very* wrong of her, and I expect he lost his temper and killed her in a fit of jealous passion.'

Triona shivered. The cold was creeping over her, chilling her blood.

'But if he was guilty, why is he now free?'

'Well it seems there was not enough evidence to bring a case in court, but of course everyone was *perfectly* certain he had done it. Some people even said they did not blame him, but that was not at all right, was it? I mean, even if his wife had been unfaithful . . . Oh dear!' She looked at the little watch hanging from a fob on her bodice. 'I didn't know it was so late. I must fly! We are dining out tonight.' She sprang up. '*How* kind of you to let me descend upon you, dear Mrs Brooks. You and your husband really *must* dine with us one night before we leave.'

Triona escorted her to her carriage and watched her drive away. Her eyes were dark and wide and her thoughts in turmoil. Elsie was a gossip; she must be mistaken. She had heard some garbled account of the tragedy and embroidered on it to satisfy her love of producing a sensation. It was not possible Duncan Ross could be a murderer, even if given cause. Elsie had said there had not been sufficient evidence to pin the crime on him. Then who had killed his wife?

Suddenly she felt she could not rest until she knew more. She told Sam to bring the carriage and drive her into town. She did not take notice of the jolting along the rough road, or the dust. All her thoughts were fixed upon Elsie's revelation.

Norah Grantley was at home, and welcomed her heartily.

'My dear Mrs Brooks—no, I shall call you Triona, it's such a pretty name, and I hope you'll call me Norah— I'm delighted to see you. We have not met lately and I've missed you. Now, what have you been doing with yourself . . .' She broke off, as her eyes rested on Triona's tense face. 'My dear, you're upset about something. What is it? Can I help you? Sit down and take your hat off and take your time telling me.'

Triona obeyed and felt herself relax. A maid brought a bowl of water and towel and she wiped her face and hands free of dust and was refreshed.

'Mrs Grantley—Norah—I have just heard a distressing piece of news. At least it was news to me, although my—my informant says it is common knowledge here. It is that Mr Duncan Ross left Trinidad because of a tragedy, and was suspected of—of . . .'

'My dear, you must have been shocked—and I think I can guess who was your informant and what a tale the little gossip made out of it.'

'I came to you because you know Mr Ross. You are friends, are you not? I know you will tell me the truth about it.'

'I will tell you what I know,' Norah said, her face

suddenly serious. 'I was in Trinidad when the tragedy occurred. I did not meet Duncan's wife, but I knew about her; everyone did, for her behaviour was a scandal. I know it isn't nice to speak ill of the dead, but I say she was a wicked woman! She was very beautiful, and men were attracted to her and she encouraged them, although she and Duncan had not been married a year. An English boy tried to commit suicide over her and was sent home. And there was a Spanish boy who was mad about her, and a middle-aged American business-man with whom she had planned to run away. We all knew about it. She was not received at Government House, and people avoided her when her behaviour became too blatant. I don't know if she had lovers, but I suspect she did. She was a woman of unbridled passion and she met a terrible end, but I shall always say she brought it upon herself.'

'Ross was suspected, but not accused of the murder, I believe.'

'That is right. There was no real evidence against him. He said that he had been out fishing with some of his boys and came back to find her dead. Of course people said he could have bribed his boys, but it could not be proved that he was anywhere near his bungalow that night. The inquest finding was murder by person or persons unknown, but it couldn't stop the gossip, and Duncan left the colony and came to Ste-Martine.'

Triona moved restlessly. 'Do *you* think he was guilty?'

Norah looked out of the window where two scraggy hens were scratching in a bed of calla lilies.

'They're loose again, the wretches,' she said irrelevantly. 'They'll ruin that bed.' She turned to look at Triona as she sat tense and waiting. 'For myself, I'm certain Duncan is not a murderer. His boys swore he was out fishing that night, and they were believed. But there were others who weren't so sure. A jealous lover could have done it, but, if he did, he managed to get away.'

Triona said slowly. 'Duncan Ross is a hard man, and if he were driven by jealousy . . . if he loved his wife passionately . . .'

'Well, all things are possible, but it's my idea that Duncan's love for his wife had been too sorely tried to last long. He buried himself in his work and they were seldom seen together.'

'He could still be jealous—and there was his pride.'

'Yes, he's a proud man, and he must have suffered greatly.' She sighed. 'But he was not formally accused, and people here have no right to treat him as if he had been. Duncan has a temper, I admit, and if his wife were unfaithful he might beat her, but not kill her. But he doesn't help himself, you know. He's brusque and un-friendly and has crushed any attempts to be social. Must you go, my dear?'

'I am afraid so.' Triona gathered up her hat and parasol. 'I shall call for Colin at the club to see whether he would change his mind and come back with me.'

'Let me send my boy with a message for him to come here,' Norah urged. 'Then we can have a chat about happier things than a past tragedy.'

For a moment Triona hesitated. If Colin had not recovered his temper, it might be best if she sent a message rather than seek him out. A dull weariness had taken hold of her and her head was aching. She thanked Norah, and sat back to listen to a description of the insolent behaviour of one of the maids who had her own ideas about how the furniture should be polished.

A shadow fell across her and she looked up to see the coloured boy at the window, bobbing his head at his mistress. 'I been to de club, ma'am, and dey say Mr Brooks ain't been dere all day.'

'Not there?' Triona repeated, surprised. 'But he said . . . Oh, I expect he has called upon someone.' She got up quickly. Was it her fancy or had a curious expression flicked across her friend's face? 'Goodbye, Norah, and thank you for letting me talk to you.'

'Ah, never thank me, my dear, but come to me whenever there is something on your mind.'

Where was Colin? The question teased her on the drive back. Probably he had changed his mind and gone elsewhere, down to the docks to watch cargo being unloaded, or perhaps he had sought out Juan Geira to discuss the fishing tackle he had been talking about recently.

She had a lonely supper and afterwards began a letter to her aunt. But she soon gave it up, finding she could not concentrate upon it. She threw a light shawl around her shoulders and went out into the cool garden. Night had fallen, and the cicadas chirped ceaselessly and palm leaves rustled softly above her as she strolled. The moon was throwing pale light that made the shadows black and mysterious. Something moved in the darkness on her left, and she heard a soft laugh. She stopped to call, 'Who is there?' Silence answered her, and she walked on.

When she went back, she called to Lara to bring her a lime drink.

Melia appeared. 'Lara done gone visit her auntie, ma'am. She ask can she go for the night if she come back early to make breakfast. You was not here, ma'am, so I say she can go. Has I done right, ma'am?'

'Oh yes, as long as she comes back early tomorrow.'

Sleep did not come for a long time. She lay listening to the sounds of the tropical night, unable to banish from her thoughts all she had heard from Elsie and Norah. She did not like Duncan Ross and she considered his behaviour unforgivable. Again she heard his muttered words: 'a woman of flame . . . a flame that can burn a man.' He had no right to speak to her, a married woman, in such a manner! It was anger, justified anger and disgust, she told herself, that brought the blood to her face as she remembered and set her body tingling!

At last she got up, feeling thirsty, and went to the table where a jug of water was kept. Something made her look out of the window and she saw a slim figure glide out from the shadows. Before it disappeared around the house, moonlight caught it and Triona saw it was Lara.

'But why has she come back now?' was her first thought. The girl had asked leave to be away for the night. Suddenly she recalled the smothered laugh she had heard earlier, and she frowned. If the girl had a lover and was meeting him secretly, she would have to go. Was this what Duncan Ross had meant when he had advised her to send the girl away?

She went back to bed and fell into uneasy sleep.

A sound awoke her. Colin had returned. She heard his stealthy footsteps pass her door and enter the other bedroom. Had he been drinking, or was he just being thoughtful in not wishing to disturb her? She waited until all was silent again.

Colin did not appear for breakfast, and Triona had hers alone, served by Lara. She looked at the girl's smooth face and impassive almond eyes as she placed coffee, pawpaw and bread upon the table.

'I believe you visited your aunt last night, Lara.'

'Yes, ma'am. Melia give me leave to go. Was it right, ma'am?'

'Yes, as long as you did not neglect your work. I believe you spent the night with your aunt. Does she live far?'

'In Regina, ma'am. I stay with her the night and come back early to do my work.'

So the girl was a liar. By now, Triona knew that most servants lied, and giggled cheerfully when found out. But there had been something curiously furtive about the slim figure flitting from the shadows last night that made her uneasy. This girl was different from the awkward, well-meaning Amy. She had a self-confidence missing in the negro servants. She was pretty and graceful—and she knew it.

When Colin appeared, she sent for fresh coffee.

'I paid a visit to Norah Grantley yesterday,' she told him. 'Did you have a pleasant time at the club?'

The moment the words were out of her mouth, she regretted them. It was a trap to catch Colin and she would have given much to recall her words, but it was too late.

He looked up. 'Oh yes, I met some fellows and had supper there. I was a bit late, so I slept in the other room rather than waken you.'

She felt her heart sink. It was her own fault; she had no right to pry into how he spent his time. She sought another subject, and asked, 'Have you found someone to take our overseer's place? It is unfortunate that Big Jim wishes to leave us.'

'I shall not be sorry to let him go,' Colin remarked. 'He's too stuck in his old ways. I have my eye on a man who is more open to new ideas. His name is Lew Corby, and he has excellent references. He's half-white, and comes from South America.'

Triona looked up sharply. 'Is he tall, with a scar on one cheek?'

'Yes, have you seen him?'

'Norah Grantley pointed him out to me one day.' She did not repeat her friend's words about the tall, narrow-eyed man lounging outside Juan Geira's store: 'That is Lew Corby, a half-caste who likes to think himself white. His reputation is not good. I have never liked his looks.'

'I suppose you will find fault with my choice as usual.' Colin's voice roused her. He had pushed his coffee aside and was staring at her, a faint flush on his face. His eyes looked heavy and angry, and suddenly she felt she could sit no longer without her own temper being aroused. She rose and went into the kitchen to discuss the day's meals with Melia.

A little later the washer-woman came to her. 'I don't find master's shirt and pants dis day, ma'am. Dey isn't dere.'

'Oh,' Triona remembered. 'They will be in the other bedroom. I'll fetch them.'

Colin's clothes lay in a heap on the floor. As she picked them up, she smelt rum and saw the stains on the shirt and dropped them in disgust. So he had been drinking in Frank Cunha's disreputable little rum shop again! Lying and drinking . . . What insidious degeneration was driving Colin to ruin? If they could talk frankly with each other; if only she could find a way to help him. Impulsively she ran from the room.

'Colin, I want . . .' she paused abruptly. Colin was standing holding a letter, and his face made her cry out, 'Oh Colin, dear, what is it? Who is it from?'

'Edward,' his voice cracked. 'My father is dead!'

'Oh, how terrible!' She went to put her arms round him, but he pushed her aside roughly. 'How did it happen?'

'His heart. It was sudden.' He had gone dead white, and his lips twitched.

'I am so dreadfully sorry.'

'You will be more sorry when you know what else my dear brother writes to say.' The bitterness in his voice chilled her, and she drew back. 'He informs me that by my father's Will everything is left to him!' The words seemed to choke him. 'I am not to receive a penny! I am to be cut off as if I were a criminal!' He flung the letter from him.

Dismay filled Triona's heart, but she felt little surprise. She had always known Edward was the favourite son.

'You do not know the worst of it,' Colin's voice roughened with fury. 'Edward writes that, in consequence of what he calls my father's generous treatment in saving me from serious financial trouble, the estate has been seriously depleted, and as he himself is about to marry, he finds himself unable to continue the allowance my father promised me!'

Triona caught her breath in dismay. She picked up the black-edged letter, and as she read the unctuous phrases, her eyes began to blaze with indignation.

'We shall do without his money! It would be unbearable to be under obligation to such a man as Edward!'

Colin rounded upon her. 'Are you a fool, Triona? Do you not see we are ruined? We have no money, no hope of ever making a living on this stinking little island!'

'We shall make Forest pay in time,' she said stoutly. 'There is much we can do, many more crops we can plant which will quickly mature and bring us in an income. And we have the money from the cocoa.' Something in his face arrested her attention. 'Colin, we *do* have that money, don't we?'

'Yes . . . of course . . . At least, some of it,' he mumbled uneasily. 'I—I have to have something to help me endure this miserable life. If I can do some sailing . . . and fishing . . . Frank knew of a small yacht going cheap.'

'Colin, you have not bought it?' she cried, appalled.

'Good heavens!' he cried, his face scarlet and furious. 'It is my money, isn't it? I'm master here and I do what I think fit! You want me to work myself into the grave! You cannot understand how I feel! You never think of how I suffer! And *you* had the effrontery to accuse me of being selfish! You have sadly changed, Triona! Sometimes I do not understand you.'

She turned away quickly. How far apart had they drifted, that they could not share misfortune when it came. They were becoming strangers to each other. She looked at him.

'Colin . . .'

'I'm going out!' He brushed past her, and she heard him racing to the stables, calling to Sam. This time she knew for certain he would return to Frank Cunha's rum shop.

CHAPTER
SEVEN

COLIN DID not return that night, or the day after. Triona became aware of the servants' curious glances and at last she sent for Ram only to be told he was missing. The news dismayed her. She could trust Ram and had meant to send him into the town to make discreet enquiries. Now this was not possible, yet she *must* find Colin.

Was he in town? Had he—the thought chilled her— left the island in his dangerously resentful mood? She wondered anxiously what she must do. To seek him in the town herself would be to betray him. She could not go asking people if they knew where her husband was; the very idea made her wince. Norah Grantley was kind, as were the vicar and his wife, but even to them she could not reveal Colin's behaviour.

Then to whom could she turn? Even as she asked herself the question, she knew the answer. She could trust only one man to find Colin and shield him from shame—Duncan Ross.

'I shall go to him and ask his help,' she said aloud, then sprang to her feet, unable for a second to believe her ears. It was Duncan's voice, saying, 'I shan't need you further, Ram. Stay and look after your mistress.'

She heard his firm step, then the door opened and he was in the room. She looked at him, feeling a tiny quiver run along her nerves. How he dominated his surroundings. There was about this man a sense of great force held in stern control. He said abruptly, 'Your husband is all right; he is with me.'

'Oh, thank heavens. I have been so anxious. How— how did you find him?'

He looked at her as if turning something over in his mind. Intuition told her what it was, and she met his eyes squarely as she said, 'Please tell me the truth.'

He considered her as she stood before him, her eyes, so deeply blue and silken-fringed, raised to his. She was wearing a thin white house-dress, short-sleeved and low-necked. Her hair was caught in a net, but a few soft curls had escaped to frame her face, a face no longer that of a pretty girl but of a beautiful woman, resolute and courageous.

'He was on the waterfront. He had been drinking with some of Cunha's friends and there had been a fight. Someone got him away before the police came, and left him on the docks.'

'Is—Is he hurt?' she breathed.

He shook his head. 'He has a black eye and several cuts—knives come in these brawls—but nothing serious. Ram came to me when your husband didn't return.'

'And you went to look for him. Oh, thank God you did!' She put her hands to her blanched cheeks.

'Sit down,' he ordered, and she obeyed without question. 'I'll get you a drink.'

'Oh no, I hate it.'

'No doubt you do, but you'll drink it. Where's that girl?' He went to the door. 'Bring your mistress a weak rum and lime, and be quick about it.' When Lara came with the drink, he took it from her, saying, 'Pack some clothes for your master, he will be staying with me for a few days.'

'Yes, sir.' Lara's narrow eyes went inquisitively from

him to Triona before she slipped from the room.

'Now drink this.' He stood over Triona until she drank. She choked a little, and felt strength return as the spirit warmed her.

Duncan seated himself opposite her. 'I'm sorry to be so abrupt, but you looked so pale and shaken. Have you eaten today?'

'I—No, I have been too anxious.'

'How like a woman. Fainting from lack of food will do no one any good, and yourself a great deal of harm.'

'I—I suppose so. I shall go back with you and get Colin . . .'

'No.' The refusal took her aback. 'Give the man time to recover himself, he's had a rough time.'

She knew what he meant; Colin must have time in which to recover his self-respect before he faced her.

'Very well. I am more grateful than I can say, Mr Ross.' How strange that she should be saying this to the man she hoped never to speak to again. 'Colin has had a great shock. Bad news came in the English mail, news that has upset him greatly. If he had not been distracted by it, he would never have—have . . .'

'Decided to try and forget it,' he ended for her. 'He is not the first man to do it. I've done the same myself.' She saw his face tighten, and guessed where his thoughts lay. 'Do not apologise for his seeking oblivion in his own way.'

'But I am so afraid for him.' Her strength had returned and she spoke frankly. 'What has happened is a shock for him.' She paused, guessing by something in his face that Colin had revealed some, if not all, of the disaster. 'I think you know something of it, Mr Ross.'

'Yes.' He got up and began to stride to and fro, frowning thoughtfully. Suddenly he turned to her. 'What has happened is a shock for *you*, also. You will suffer—but your husband does not appear to have thought of that.'

'Oh, he does, but just now, when he is so overwrought . . .' Words failed her, and she looked away unhappily.

'You will have to make your husband face up to things, Mrs Brooks.' His voice, cool and hard, made her look swiftly at him. 'I am going to be brutally frank, and if I offend you it cannot be helped. Your husband will ruin himself if he once starts drinking seriously and keeping company with Cunha's friends. It is fatally easy for a man to give up hope and go to pieces on an island like this. Forest Estate can, in time, pay its way, but only if he will take advice and work hard.'

'But there are the workers to pay, and the servants. And the money from the cocoa is spent.' She did not ask herself why she was speaking so frankly to the man she had planned to avoid. 'Will it be possible to borrow from the bank?'

'I think so. Not a lot, but it will help the situation if they see that your husband is prepared to work the estate seriously. By the way, I've arranged for the boat your husband bought to be re-sold. He has agreed to it.'

'Thank you,' she said wearily. She rose to her feet. 'Mr Ross, will you try to make Colin see how necessary it is that he sets to work at once? He does not always listen to what I say, and indeed I do not know much about the management of an estate, I fear.'

He paused in his restless pacing to face her. There was a strange look on his lean face, and his eyes blazed with a sudden light that made her step back quickly, startled.

'You wish me to save him from destroying himself, the man who isn't worthy of you? A man who thinks only of himself and does not cherish a woman who is worth twenty of him? A man who will never . . .'

'Stop!' She flung out her hands as if to ward off a blow.

'You shall not talk of him like that! You judge all men by yourself; you demand they shall be as hard and ruthless as you! Life had not been easy for Colin, and he has suffered . . .' Sudden memory checked her torrent of angry words. The man standing before her had suffered, and most cruelly. Innocent or guilty, his life held tragedy and pain. Her anger died as swiftly as it had risen, and she turned away with a heavy sigh. 'I am sorry; I should not have spoken so. Please forget it. I must see if Lara has packed what is necessary.'

'Wait.' He caught her arm as she turned away. 'I shall not take back what I have said—but I should not have said it. When I see you growing pale and thin from anxiety . . .' He drew a deep breath and released her. 'I shall do what I can, since you ask me, and I shall bring him back the day after tomorrow.'

'Thank you. I am deeply grateful for what you have done for Colin.'

An odd smile touched his lips for a moment. 'You think I did it for him?' He went out of the room, calling to Lara to bring the case of clothes.

Triona sank into a chair, relief flooding over her. Colin was safe and being looked after.

Sleep came quickly and dreamlessly to her that night, and she awoke feeling refreshed and energetic. After she had dealt with household matters she went out to speak to Ram. The gardener's manner, as always, was respectful and calm as they discussed sweet potatoes, yams, dasheens and eddoes.

'The earth is good,' he told her, picking up a handful and letting it trickle through his brown fingers. 'Many things will grow in it. I will plant much and there will be much to send to market.'

So he had guessed how necessary it was to bring in some money, however little it might be.

She said, 'That will be useful, Ram.'

He turned to stare at the wooded hills rising behind the plantation. 'You have good mahogany trees, mistress, in your forest. The wood makes good furniture, many people pay much money for it.'

'But who would buy it from me, Ram?'

'Mr Juan Geira buys it. He have a son in St Lucia making chairs and tables, he will buy mahogany for his son.'

'How would I get the trees cut?'

'I find men.'

'Thank you, Ram, I shall discuss it with Mr Brooks.'

After lunch she busied herself putting great vases of flowers throughout the house, plumbago, bougainvillaea, canna lilies. Melia was told to prepare Colin's favourite dish, pastelles, meat mixed with corn-meal and spices and wrapped in a banana-leaf, and Sam was sent into town to see if any English mail had arrived.

She refused to allow herself to speculate on what Colin's mood would be when he came back. She would allow nothing to distress her. Colin needed her help.

She had finished dinner and was sitting under a lamp doing some sewing when a sound made her look up, and for a moment her nerves tightened. A man was at the veranda window, a tall, pale-brown man with a thin, watchful face and a scar on one cheek. He bowed when she looked at him and said in a soft, faintly unpleasant voice,

'Good evening, Mrs Brooks. I am Lew Corby. Can I speak with Mr Brooks, please?'

'My husband is away,' she told him, disliking the way he was staring at her. She had loosened her hair from the chignon net and it lay around her shoulders. 'Come to see him next week.'

'Mr Brooks is away tonight?' A smile creased the

man's cheeks, and suddenly she felt a prick of fear. He had perched on the edge of the window and she thought he was going to swing himself into the room. 'That is indeed too bad. I wished to see him. You must be feeling lonely, Mrs Brooks.'

She rose quickly. 'Goodnight. I shall tell Mr Brooks you will see him next week.'

He did not move, but continued to stare at her, at the thin muslin gown she wore in the evenings, her bare neck and arms and the cascade of brilliant hair. She was abruptly cold and tense. The servants were in their quarters some way off. She said sharply, 'You may go!'

Instead of leaving, he slid one leg over the window-frame, then turned round at the sound of a soft step. Ram stood where the lamplight caught his slim figure. He stood quite still, gently swinging the cutlass he held.

The man gave a little hiss of laughter and slid off the window and bowed.

'Goodnight, Mrs Brooks. I shall come again.'

He moved away into the shadows, and Triona let out the breath she had been holding.

'Ram, what do you know of this man called Lew Corby?'

'I do not know him, mistress, I only hear things of him.'

'What sorts of things?'

'Many things, and not good.' Then he, too, was lost in the shadows.

She went to the windows and let down the wooden shutters. For a brief moment she had known fear and her heart was still beating fast. She recalled Norah's words: 'That is Lew Corby . . . his reputation is not good . . .'

This was the man Colin wanted to hire as overseer. But when he knew of his reputation and his visit tonight, he would send him away.

That night, before she got into bed, she went to the window. A slim figure moved silently through the shadows and she caught the gleam of steel; the gardener was keeping watch, and she could sleep peacefully.

On the morning of Colin's return, Lara came to tell Triona that Juan Geira was outside and wished to speak to her. When she came out, he bowed, sweeping his battered hat from his head when he saw her.

'Forgive me for taking your time, Señora Brooks. Ram Takoor tells me you have some fine mahogany trees you are wishing to sell. I shall be gratified to buy them from you at a good price if the trees are matured.'

'I shall ask my husband about it,' she told him, liking his courteous manner. His clothes were worn and not over-clean, but he bore himself with a dignity that was somehow impressive. She wondered what had been his life before coming to Ste-Martine to be a storekeeper. 'I shall let you know his decision. I believe you have a son in St Lucia who makes furniture.'

He bowed. 'That is so. He works cleverly and often I buy wood for him. I wish you a good morning, Señora Brooks.'

At noon she heard the sound of carriage and flew to the window to see Colin getting out of Ross's buggy. When he entered the room, she ran into his arms.

'Colin, dearest, I have been so anxious about you! Let me look at you.'

She leaned back in the circle of his arms to look up into his face, and saw with solicitude the ugly bruise over one eye and cut on one cheek.

'I am perfectly all right, Triona. Pray do not fuss so.' He let her go and sank into a chair and wiped his face with a handkerchief, not looking at her. 'It's damned hot today.'

'I'll get you something cool to drink,' she said quickly.

'Lime or orange . . .' She broke off as Lara came into the room with a tray holding a bottle of rum and a glass. 'No, Lara, that is not what I want. Take it away.'

'It is what master wants.' There was veiled insolence in the girl's voice as she put the tray beside Colin. 'He ask me for it.'

Triona waited until the girl had left. Then she said, picking up the bottle, 'It is too early in the day for rum, Colin. Lime will be much more cooling.'

'Leave it there!' Colin's demand startled her. 'God knows I've been through a bad time and I need something to put some life into me.' He avoided her eye as he poured out the spirit. 'I asked the girl to bring it.'

She went to the window and stared unseeingly out at the vivid green and scarlet of the poinsettias bordering the path. Suddenly she heard a groan and turned to see Colin, his drink untouched and his head in his hands.

'I've been a fool, Triona! Edward's letter . . . I think I went a little crazy when I knew we might starve. I went to Frank's, and there was a fight . . .'

'I know about it, Colin. Thank God that Mr Ross and Ram found you. It is all over and we shall not speak of it. Things will not be as bad as you fear.'

She began to tell him about selling the mahogany trees to Juan Geira, and her heart rose when he showed enthusiasm for the idea. He too had plans for growing arrowroot and other crops, plans which she guessed had been suggested by Duncan Ross.

It was late that evening, when the air was delightfully cool and the nightly chorus of cicadas had begun, when Colin said suddenly, 'I am going to write to your Aunt Jane. While your father was alive, she received money for your keep, and she can't have used it all. You said you lived in a very small way. I expect she invested it and is now enjoying the income. I think it is only fair she should help us now. Anyway, I consider you have a right to the money.'

Triona dropped her sewing in dismay. 'Oh no, Colin. I do not think my father ever sent very much, and I suspect there were times when he sent nothing. And, once he had died, she had to bear all the expense of my education. It may well be that she had to borrow money which she is now repaying.'

'Damn!' Colin snapped irritably. 'I had counted on getting something out of her. If she is so devoted to you, she could spare us something, couldn't she?'

Triona rose swiftly. Despite the coolness of the evening, she felt she was stifling. Colin sat hunched in his chair, his handsome young features brooding and sullen. A feeling of helplessness came over her, taking away much of her pleasure at his return. Murmuring that she was tired, she went to bed and, when he came up, she pretended to be asleep.

Several days passed before she brought up the matter of Lew Corby. Colin was more cheerful. He had gone to town and returned fairly certain he would be able to borrow money from the bank.

'Colin, I wish you would not engage that man Corby as overseer. I don't like or trust him. Please send him away if he comes.'

He stared at her, frowning. 'What has got into your head now, Triona? The man has some education and experience, and I shall certainly hire him.'

'Please don't, Colin. He came here when I was alone and he—he frightened me. His manner was most impertinent and I was relieved when Ram came. Norah Grantley once told me he had a bad reputation.'

'I do not wish to know what old Mrs Gossip told you, or what silly fancies you have. Who else do you wish me to dismiss, the cook?'

'No, only Lara.' She met his angry gaze calmly. 'I have decided I don't like her, and I suspect she is dishonest. I have missed things lately. She is also a liar, and I shall send her away.'

'You will do nothing of the kind!' Colin had risen, his face scarlet. '*I* am master here and I say the girl remains! Your head is full of mad notions these days—you suspect everyone! You shall not dictate to me. The girl stays!'

He left the room, leaving Triona fighting to control the blaze of anger that swept over her like a flame, a flame that burned away excuses for Colin's behaviour and left her with the stark fact that the man she loved and had married was being lost in the restless, moody, frustrated man whose furious words seemed to hang in the air.

Melia put her head in at the door. 'Mistress Grantley coming, ma'am. I think she visit with you.'

Triona pulled her scattered thoughts together. 'Then tell Lara to bring coffee.'

'I bring it self, ma'am.'

'Why?' Triona asked sharply. 'Where is Lara?'

The cook shrugged her plump shoulders. 'She done go somewheres, ma'am. I bring coffee.'

Norah came into the room and, with her, it seemed to Triona, came something calm and cheerful and matter of fact.

'I'm here to invite you and your husband to a dinner-party tomorrow,' she said, sinking into a chair. 'It is disgracefully short notice, but the Claytons have been recalled suddenly, and Archie Hallam is off on the same boat, and I'm giving a little farewell dinner. You both must come.'

'How very kind of you,' Triona exclaimed. 'We should love it . . .' Suddenly she knew that Colin would not love it and would certainly refuse to go. 'But I am afraid Colin is unwell, so I feel I must refuse.'

'Well, now, if that isn't too bad. What is the matter with Mr Brooks? Is it serious?'

'Oh no, just a touch of—of fever,' Triona assured her hurriedly. 'But I know he will not be able to accept your invitation.' She sighed involuntarily, thinking how pleasant it would be to get away from the house and enjoy a cheerful evening among friends.

Norah glanced shrewdly at her downcast face. 'Well, my dear, if your husband cannot come, and if there is no need for you to stay with him, why do you not come to me?'

'Oh, I couldn't. I mean . . .'

'You mean it isn't the conventional thing for a wife to attend a party without her husband.' Norah nodded her head. 'And quite right, too, in the case of some wives. But I have it! You must come and spend a couple of days with me, Triona, my dear. Then, as my house guest, there will be no criticism. You are looking peaky and not your true self.' Her eyes took in Triona's pale face and shadowed eyes. 'I am sure your husband will not object, and it would cheer you up.'

Triona opened her lips to make a polite refusal but, before the words could come, she heard a horse being spurred down the avenue and knew Colin had left. So he did not intend to apologise for his behaviour. For a second she hesitated, then the events of the last days seemed to rise to crush her and she said breathlessly, 'Thank you, Norah, I accept your invitation. May I come with you now? It will not take me long to pack some clothes.'

'I'm delighted, my dear. But call your maid to do the packing.'

'I would rather do it myself.' Triona sprang to her feet.

'Melia will bring you some coffee.'

'Your husband . . .'

'I shall leave a note for him,' Triona said, and ran from the room. Her heart was beating fast, and there was a bright spot of colour in each cheek.

Melia came to help after she had served coffee, and Sam carried the case down to the waiting carriage. Triona took her place beside her friend and they drove off. She had changed into a silvery grey poplin dress and her face under the shade of her rose parasol was faintly flushed and her blue eyes very bright.

Norah Grantley, observing her, thought her eyes a trifle too bright, but she was not a woman to ask questions. If a husband was left to find a wife missing and a scribbled note to explain, it could only mean he deserved it!

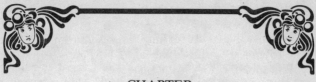

CHAPTER
EIGHT

TRIONA STOOD before the long looking-glass in Norah's guest bedroom and felt excitement stir her blood. She was not vain, but it could not be denied that tonight she was beautiful. Her dress was one of her trousseau gowns, a creamy silk trimmed with rows of pale green ruched ribbon and Brussels lace, the low-cut bodice displaying the beauty of her neck and shoulders and the skirt, frilled and swept back to a slight train, showed off her slim figure to its best advantage. She wore no jewels except the emerald earrings that had been her mother's. Her glowing hair was gathered to the top of her head with a few loose curls falling down her back. She had been about to place a small circle of silk roses and ribbon on her hair, but her hostess forbade it.

'My dear, it would be a thousand pities to hide a single curl of your lovely hair,' Norah declared as she rustled in, stiff and elegant in turquoise satin. 'Isn't it a fine thing to be as slim as a willow wand! My corset will be the death of me before the evening is over; the maid laced me so tightly I hadn't breath to tell her to stop. I must go down—the vicar and his wife are always early.'

Triona joined her in the long cool sitting-room just as the Rev. Ernest Fisher and his wife were shown in by the negro butler. Mrs Fisher went up to her hostess and asked in a quiet voice,

'Is he coming?'

'He is,' Norah answered in the same tone. 'Am I making a mistake, d'you think?'

'No indeed, you are being both courageous and kind, which is what we all should be if we are true Christians.'

'Well, there will be some Christians tonight who may not think as we do,' Norah remarked, fanning herself. 'Ah well, a shock is good for us all.' She turned to greet the Claytons and two other couples who had entered.

A few minutes later Archie Hallam arrived and, after greeting his hostess, came up to Triona, saying eagerly, 'Mrs Brooks! I have not seen you lately.'

'I have not been in town much,' she said, smiling at his obvious boyish admiration. 'I believe you are leaving Ste-Martine very shortly.'

'Unfortunately, yes. I had hoped to be here much longer. I hate to go, you know.'

He was interrupted by Mr Fisher, who wished to direct Triona's attention to the view over the town where lights pricked the darkness like glow-worms.

Voices and laughter soon filled the room. Triona's thoughts went to Colin returning to find her gone. Would he be angry? Or would he be secretly grateful to have time in which to let their differences be forgotten and forgiven? She pulled her mind away from thoughts that could only pain her, determined to enjoy herself tonight. Suddenly she heard the butler saying, 'Mr Ross, ma'am,' and, turning swiftly, she stared as others were staring at the man standing in the doorway.

For a moment he stood looking at the faces turned to him, his grey eyes cool and impersonal, his lean face inscrutable. Then he walked to his hostess, who came to meet him and gave him her hand as she looked up into his face.

'It's good to see you, Duncan. We don't meet you often enough, you know.'

'I'm a busy man,' he told her, smiling. The smile changed his face in a startling way, and Triona, watching him, realised how little he smiled.

'Well, you know everyone here, I think,' Norah said, as the Fishers came forward to claim Ross's attention.

Triona stood opening and shutting her fan, not hearing Archie Hallam's voice beside her. In that moment when Ross stood in the doorway, their eyes had met and she had felt an abrupt, breathless shock that had shaken her and left her disturbed yet oddly excited. So Ross was the 'he' about whom Mrs Fisher had asked. She had praised Norah for her bravery in bringing the man so often ignored into her party. How would he be received, Triona wondered uneasily?

She glanced at the people around her. They had resumed their chatter and several men were talking to Ross. The women looked uncertain, and a few were exchanging meaning glances. She turned to Archie Hallam.

'I am pleased to see Mr Ross here tonight. He does not often go into society.'

'Well—er—no, he doesn't.' Archie Hallam was obviously uncomfortable. 'I mean, he doesn't care to meet people, I gather. He's a clever chap; makes a good thing out of his estate.'

'*What* a surprise—and *how* like dear Norah!' A pinch on her arm made Triona turn to meet Elsie Clayton's amused eyes. 'She is always perfectly oblivious to what people think. Really, it is interesting to see him in evening dress; he looks quite distinguished. You know, I have never spoken to him.'

'Then you must let me introduce him to you,' Triona suggested drily.

'Oh dear, I think you had better not, Mrs Brooks, my husband would not care for it, I fear.' Elsie fluttered her fan, causing her fair frizzled hair to dance about her face. 'I mean—Well, he is not received everywhere, is he?'

'We have reason to be grateful to Mr Ross,' Triona said coolly. 'He has been most helpful in advising us on many things. We came here without any knowledge of life and work on an estate.'

'Oh yes, he would do that, I'm sure. But, well, you know what I told you . . .'

'I think it is possible truth has been obscured by rumour. No one should judge another until the whole truth is known.'

Elsie shrugged. 'But truth is so difficult to discover— and rumour is so *much* more amusing!' She smiled and drifted away.

'I don't think that is a very pleasant thing to say,' Archie Hallam said, frowning. 'Nothing was proved against Ross. *Someone* killed his unfortunate wife, but it could have been a marauder, or . . .' He glanced at her, obviously wondering how much she had heard.

'She was about to run away with another man,' Triona said bluntly.

'How could he know she was going to?'

'She left a letter.'

'And the letter was there for all the world to see.' He looked thoughtful. 'You know, if *I* had killed my wife, I wouldn't have left a letter like that lying about afterwards. It could help to pin the crime on me. A betrayed husband might act in sudden passion, you know.'

She stared at him. 'Why—I never thought of that! It was evidence against him; it gave a reason why he might wish to kill her.'

'But he *didn't* destroy it, probably because he wasn't there.'

'Then you believe him innocent?'

'Yes, I do.' Archie Hallam's young face was suddenly

serious. 'I think it's a wretched shame that he has been saddled with a suspicion that may ruin his life. People are pretty unkind sometimes, you know.'

Impulsively she laid her hand on his arm. 'But *you* are not unkind, Mr Hallam, and I like you for it.'

He blushed deeply as he stammered, 'That's—That's frightfully nice of you, Mrs Brooks. It means a lot to me that you should say that.'

'Good evening, Mrs Brooks,' Ross's deep voice broke in on the young man's words. 'I don't see your husband here.'

'He has a little fever and does not feel inclined for society tonight,' she said, a little breathlessly. She looked down at the fan she held, her long lashes brushing her cheeks that had grown suddenly warm. 'He is not perfectly adjusted to the climate here yet, I fear.' She looked up. 'Do you know Mr Hallam?'

He bowed slightly. 'I have not had the honour. But I am afraid my acquaintance with him must unfortunately be cut short, as our hostess has sent me with a message that she wishes to claim Mr Hallam.'

'Oh dear—then I must go to her.' Archie Hallam looked wistfully at Triona. 'I hoped I might have the pleasure of taking you in to dinner . . .'

'I'm sorry to disappoint you,' Ross said. 'But that honour is to be mine tonight.' He watched the young man walk away, and added, 'Your young admirer must learn to disguise his disappointment better; it makes him vulnerable.'

'Is it so bad to be vulnerable?' Triona asked, looking up at him.

'Bad and dangerous,' he said briefly. 'Is your husband truly sick with the fever?'

'No, but I felt certain he would not wish to come tonight.'

'You felt certain? Did you ask him?'

She hesitated, but knew it was no use trying to hide the truth. 'I did not ask him, because he had gone out. Mrs Grantley was most anxious for me to visit her for two days, and she was one lady short for her dinner-table.'

He stroked his chin, considering her thoughtfully. 'I—see. Does he know you are here?'

'But of course he does!' Her eyes flashed dangerously. 'Naturally, I left him a note telling him where I had gone.'

'Oh, of course,' he agreed smoothly, but mockery lay under his words, and she turned away abruptly, suddenly wishing she had not accepted Norah's invitation. Probably people were thinking it strange she should be present without her husband. Meeting Duncan Ross had shaken her more than she cared to admit. Without looking at him, she knew his eyes were on her with an expression that brought her a feather touch of fear.

Was she afraid of this harsh, forceful man? She flinched from the thought, forcing herself to smile and say lightly, 'How charmingly Mrs Grantley arranges her flowers. Her parties are always delightful.'

'I hate dinner-parties, as I think you must know. I came only because you were here. Norah told me she was determined to get you away for a few days.'

Triona caught her breath. 'But why? Does she know. . . Does everyone know?'

'Not from me, and not much. But in a small island like this, gossip is rife, I'm afraid,' he told her, frowning. 'We all suffer.' He shrugged. 'Don't let it worry you. Something else will catch the attention of people; it is mostly the women who have too little to do and to think about. Norah is signalling to us. I'm afraid you will have to put up with me as your dinner-partner. I'm sorry if it is not to your liking.'

He did not look as if he was sorry. He offered her his arm and they proceeded sedately towards the dining-room. Triona knew many eyes were upon them and she held her head high, pretending not to notice. She would not have chosen Duncan Ross as her dinner-partner, but since Norah had allotted him to her she did not intend to appear discomposed or embarrassed.

Conversation flowed around her, ranging from the price of copra, a suspected case of the dreaded coffee-bug and England's proposed Elementary Education Act to the behaviour of Mrs Fisher's cook, who appeared for work wearing a crinoline.

Triona talked to Mr Fisher, but she was very conscious of Ross on her other side. She wondered if he had this effect on other people. He was silent much of the time, but when someone asked him a question she saw how heads were turned to hear his reply. His very reticence among the chattering guests drew attention to him. Under cover of the talk around them, he turned to ask beneath his breath,

'Is your husband recovered?'

'Yes, but he is in a very bad temper.'

His dark brows rose. 'But not with you, surely?'

'I'm afraid we had—a little disagreement.' Once again she was telling him more than she meant to. 'That is really why I came away. He will have got over it by the time I return. He has been speaking about plans for the estate and ideas you have put to him. I am grateful to you.'

'I am glad if I have been of any help.' His tone was formal, and he turned to speak to the woman on his other side.

Triona was glad when the evening was over, although it had been a good dinner and she had met and enjoyed talking to people after the isolation of Forest Estate.

Archie Hallam's obvious devotion touched and amused her, but she was not sad about his imminent departure. He would, no doubt, fall in love with someone on the home trip and soon forget her.

Ross came over to Triona, who was sitting alone by a window.

'I want to see your husband about clearing some of his land—he has asked my advice. I'll come over to Forest sometime soon.'

'Thank you,' she said. 'I know he will be pleased to see you.'

'I wonder if *you* will be pleased?' He lowered his voice as he spoke. 'Young Hallam's no fool to fall in love with the most beautiful woman he has ever met.' His eyes swept her from her crown of burnished hair to her little satin slippers. 'Thank God you don't drape your head with feathers and ribbons. Your hair is a glory that must not be hidden, Triona.'

She looked away from his intent eyes, and said lightly, 'Thank you for the compliment, Mr Ross.'

'Great heavens, woman, don't you know truth from a compliment?' He turned abruptly and, going up to Norah, bade her a brief farewell before striding from the room.

When Triona was in her bedroom, preparing to undress, Norah came in, her loose wrapper and comfortable curves proclaiming release from her stays.

'I couldn't have stood them a minute longer,' she confided, to Triona's amusement. 'Isn't it terrible what we women will do in the name of fashion?' She dropped into a chair. 'Did the evening go well, d'you think?'

'Oh, very well indeed,' Triona assured her. 'The dinner was delightful, and your servants are so well trained. I am sure everyone had a charming evening.'

'What did you think of my devilment in getting Duncan to come?' She gave a chuckle. 'The cat among the pigeons—And good for the pigeons, I'd say. It's time people took their minds off the past and showed charity to a man who has been cruelly treated and, to my belief, with no reason at all.'

Triona began to pull the pins out of her hair. 'I'm not sure Mr Ross will welcome any charity. He appears to do very well without it.'

'Ah, that's his pride, my dear. He's a lonely man, and I'm sorry for him. He came because I told him you were coming, did you know that? I'm glad you've brought some interest into his life.' She was silent for some minutes, watching the thick curling hair tumble down Triona's back. 'My dear, any woman would give her eyes to have hair like yours. But take care; my husband used to say a woman with your shade of hair meant danger for herself and for others.' She heaved herself out of the chair with a sigh. 'Ah well, I could have done with a bit more danger myself. Goodnight to you, and happy dreams.'

Norah took her guest to visit friends in the cool of the morning, and on the way back she stopped the carriage in the town.

'I must speak to Juan Geira about some guavas he is getting for me to make jelly.'

'He is a strange man,' Triona remarked. 'I have wondered about him. He is not the usual type of storekeeper, I think.'

'That's true enough,' Norah agreed. 'I've often thought he might be someone who was once of importance. Drink, perhaps, brought him down, or some political trouble that made him leave Spain.'

By the end of the day Triona had become restless. She did not like to suggest she return home that night, but decided she would go early in the afternoon next day. Norah tried to persuade her to stay another night, but desisted when she saw Triona was determined to leave. She made no mention of what she had probably heard about Colin, but her eyes were anxious when she bade Triona goodbye the next day.

'It's been a great joy to have had you, my dear. Now, don't forget, you're to come to me if . . . Well, whenever you have the notion. You'll always be welcome.'

Triona kissed her warmly, thanking her for all her kindness, and she was driven away in the Grantley carriage. But her pleasure slowly became shadowed by wondering in what mood she would find Colin. She told herself it was natural for him to take some time to recover from his unfortunate experience and she must be patient and understanding.

There was no sign of life when she went into the house. The servants had disappeared into their quarters in the noonday heat. Colin would probably be taking a siesta if he were not out on the estate.

She went softly into their bedroom, so as not to waken him if he slept, and opened the door. Ice-cold with horror, she saw the two naked bodies, white and golden-skinned, entwined on the bed!

Her gasp made them break apart. Lara's sleek hair lay across Colin's shoulders as he turned to stare. Rigid with shock, Triona watched alarm, shame and anger cross his face. He tried to speak, failed, then stammered stupidly,

'I . . . you said you would return tonight . . .'

Shock had numbed her, but now, with the sudden, fierce intensity of a forest fire, her anger burst into flame. A few steps took her to the girl cowering behind Colin. Her hand grasped the silky black hair, and the girl whimpered as she was dragged from the bed!

'*Get out!*' Triona did not recognise her voice as she

spat the words out. 'You filthy little beast! Get out and never show your face here again, do you hear me?'

Lara crawled away from her, moaning, and then, springing to her feet, ran from the room.

Colin had risen, aghast at her violence, and she knew he was afraid. 'Triona . . . Don't . . . I didn't mean . . .'

'You did not mean me to discover you!' She flung the words at him. 'How long has she been your mistress? When did you first seduce her?'

'I didn't. Please be reasonable about this, Triona.'

'You ask me to be *reasonable*?'

'She seduced *me*, I swear it. She wasn't a virgin. She had been old Smith's mistress until he threw her out. She faked that reference she gave you. She began hanging around me trying to . . . She isn't like the other girls. I—I found her sexually attractive. And then you went off without telling me! Oh yes, you left a note, just like a woman who leaves her husband for good! You went off to enjoy yourself and flirt with that damned little puppy, Hallam! Yes, I knew he was there, and I know Ross was there, too. And I can guess why.' His voice took on a note of outrage that sickened her. 'I've seen how he looks at you—and I don't believe you when you say you don't like him! He has visited the house when I wasn't here . . .' He broke off, frightened by what he read in her face. 'Triona, don't look at me like that! I—I'm sorry for what happened. I promise you it won't happen again. I'll send the girl away.'

'I should never have engaged her. Duncan—Mr Ross—told me to send her away. Now I know why.'

Colin's face was suddenly flushed with fury. 'What damned business is it of his whom I employ? You are making a rather ridiculous fuss about something relatively unimportant, Triona.' He avoided looking at her as he spoke. 'You must know by now that most of the men living in these tropical climates take native girls occasionally. It is the life they have to live . . . It doesn't mean anything.'

Triona watched him pick up a towel and wrap it round his waist and brush back the hair clinging to his sweating forehead. Her anger had died, burned out in that one furious flame of shock and loathing. What was left, she wondered? Pity? Memory of first happiness and love? The man before her was not the man she had once loved. She closed her eyes for a moment in anguish at the truth that could no longer be denied.

Colin said restlessly, 'You're being so hard, Triona. I've been very wrong, I know, but it is your duty as my wife to understand and forgive.'

She was suddenly calm, empty of all emotion. She picked up his clothes from the floor and tossed them to him.

'I do understand, and because I know you cannot help being the man you are, I can forgive you.'

'That is not what a loving wife should say to her husband,' he shouted. 'You are behaving in a quite ridiculously wild and theatrical manner! A loving wife . . .' His bluster died as he met her eyes.

'But I am no longer a loving wife,' she said bleakly.

'Triona . . . You cannot mean that you no longer love me?'

'I despise you. You sicken me with your whining excuses.' Her voice held a deadly finality that made him recoil before it. 'I am legally your wife, but from now on we lead separate lives. Now go.'

His face crimsoned, then turned very white, and without another word he went from the room.

CHAPTER
NINE

NEXT MORNING Triona awoke from a troubled sleep to see Melia standing by the bed with a tray.

'Master done gone out and you sleep late, so's ah think maybe you is tired and I brings you breakfast, ma'am,' the cook said. She put the tray on the bedside table and folded away the mosquito-net, studiously avoiding Triona's eyes. 'Take a nice rest, ma'am.'

Triona sat up, shaking her hair out of her eyes. She had been awake until dawn and now she felt a deep weariness of body and spirit. She looked at the cook's round, ebony face and wondered dully how much she, and others, knew of Colin's behaviour. There was little that the servants did not know of their employers' households.

'Melia, I shall tell Lara to leave. I am not pleased with her work or behaviour.'

'She done gone already, ma'am.' Melia's face was expressionless.

'Did you like her, Melia?'

'No, ma'am.' Melia looked down, her fingers pleating a corner of her apron. 'I think she a no-good girl. I glad she done gone.'

'But you never said anything, you did not complain about her or say you thought she was no good.'

'No, ma'am. I is frightened.'

'Frightened of her?' Triona asked, surprised. 'But why?'

The cook glanced swiftly over her plump shoulder before whispering,

'She a bad girl. She know *obeah*! She make bad things happen!'

Triona knew how strong the fear of *obeah* was among the natives. Illness, misfortune and death could be brought about, the African folk believed, by *obeah*, and the dread of it lay deep in their natures.

She began to pour out the coffee. 'Melia, you have a cousin; can she come and work for me?'

'Yes, ma'am, she come. She glad to work for you.'

Triona took a sip of coffee and looked up at the cook. 'It tastes different, Melia.'

The woman fixed her eyes a foot above Triona's head. 'I done put a small little drop of rum in, ma'am. It give coffee strength.' She bowed and waddled away, leaving her young mistress grateful for the kindly thought but disturbed by its implication.

Later, she rose, aware of a dragging weariness and curious numbness of mind that allowed her to think of last night without pain. Pain, she knew, would come later and shame for the man she no longer loved. Colin, once over his shock at her decree that they no longer live as man and wife, would rebel. His masculine vanity would not easily accept her statement that she no longer loved him, he would persuade himself that she was jealous of Lara and wished to make him suffer for his lapse. That night she locked her bedroom door. She heard him try the handle, then move on into the other room.

For the next few days he sulked. She knew he was waiting for her to forgive him and when this did not happen she had to put up with scenes that made her sick at heart. He continued to put all blame on her, declaring her lack of wifely sympathy had driven him to find consolation elsewhere. When at last he realised he had indeed lost her love, he became pitiful, begging her to love him again and to forgive him. As days passed, his pleas died and his face grew stony and his manner cold and brusque and he spent an increasing amount of his time in the town.

Ram came to Triona one morning to say he had men to cut the mahogany trees and that Juan Geira would arrange to collect the wood and ship it to his son in St Lucia. Since Colin now took no interest in the matter, Triona told the gardener to go ahead and cut the trees out of the woods that were part of the estate.

She had written a brief, formal letter of condolence to Edward in which she made no reference to his father's Will. Edward, she knew, would never help them, and she did not wish it.

Juan and his team loaded the cut trees on ox-carts for delivery to the docks. When he came to the house to pay her, he hesitated, shuffling his feet and looking at her with troubled eyes.

'Señora Brooks, this is not easy for me to say, but if you would think it best for me to keep some of the money for you . . . I would be gratified to be your banker, and no . . . other person need know how much I pay you.'

So he knew how Colin would spend the money if he got his hands on it. The knowledge was bitter; yet how could anyone in the colony be unaware of Colin's physical and moral decline and the shadow that had fallen on their marriage. Servants gossiped, and some of the gossip reached their employers. Perhaps they knew about Lara also. Triona had not seen the girl since that dreadful day, but she suspected she was in the town and some instinct told her that Colin was seeing her.

She accepted the situation because she could do nothing else. There was no money for her to return to England, and she knew she could not leave Colin even though her love for him was dead. She was his wife, and they had once been happy together.

Pride would not let her accept Juan's offer. She thanked him and dismissed him. She would not tell Colin the total amount the wood had brought. She would keep back enough to pay the servants and pay for food. For the first time in her life she would have to lie to Colin.

Ram had gone into the market one morning and when he returned he asked to see her. She saw, with some surprise, that his usually bland face expressed uneasiness and he seemed uncertain of how to begin speaking.

'Yes, Ram, what is it?' she asked.

His glance slid away from her. 'Mistress Brooks, I ask that you lock doors always, please.'

'Lock the doors?' she repeated in astonishment. 'What do you mean, Ram?'

'Is danger for you, mistress. Bad magic come to hurt you.' His voice had sunk to a whisper.

'Danger? Bad magic? What is this nonsense?' she demanded, more sharply than she intended because of an odd little chill of fear. Ram looked at the floor and was silent. 'Ram, tell me what you mean, do you hear? It is an order.'

'I hear.' He looked up. 'It is the girl Lara you send away. She very angry with you and say bad things. She say she put *obeah* on you and make you sick. I meet Lara in the market this day.'

'And what did you tell her when she—she threatened me?'

'I say nothing to she, I hit she down to the ground so she bawl. You keep doors locked, please?'

She nodded, ashamed of her fears. 'Very well. But I am not frightened by the girl's silly threats.'

So Lara was in town as she had suspected. The thought was not pleasant, but it was absurd to be afraid of an angry servant's threats. The negroes were firm believers in *obeah* and greatly afraid of it, and Ram, too, seemed to share some if not all of their fears. Ignorant people were much given to superstition and tribal magic, although such beliefs were discouraged by church and government.

However, she found herself locking the house doors if she was alone in the house, and always at night. Colin had a key and could let himself in when, or if, he came home.

She went to bed late one night, weary with trying to devise ways of bringing in more money from the estate. As she lay in the dark, a curious feeling of uneasiness crept over her and refused to be shaken off. Was there a faint sound in the house? She sat up, her uneasiness growing stronger. The house was locked up as usual and she had let down the shutters except those on her bedroom windows. No one could get in . . . and yet, surely she heard a faint rustle . . . a soft step . . . She must be imagining things! It was too early for Colin's return and she knew his heavy and often unsteady footsteps. She flung aside the mosquito net and went to the door, hesitated, then turned to the window. There was no moon, but starlight gave an eerie glow and she saw a figure, too dimly seen to be recognised, slip from the shadow of the house into the tangle of trees.

She told herself firmly that it was probably one of Melia's friends calling on her and there was nothing to be afraid of. The house was securely locked and . . . She started violently at a sound from outside her room!

Gathering her courage, she called, 'Who is there? Answer me!'

'Is Ram, Mistress Brooks.' His voice brought a wave of relief, and she unlocked the door to stare at him.

'What are you doing here, Ram? And how did you get in?'

'The front door unlocked, mistress.'

'But I locked it myself, and let down the shutters.'

'The front door unlocked,' he insisted. He moved away and for the first time she noticed he kept his hands behind his back. 'I go now. Please to lock the front door, mistress.'

'I don't understand. How *could* the door be unlocked?'

'Please not to worry. Everything all right now. All safe for you.' He began to back away from her into the shadows.

'Ram,' she called. 'What are you holding behind you?'

'Is nothing.' His voice came from the darkness. 'Please to lock the door.'

'But . . .' she paused, hearing his footsteps fade, feeling puzzled and apprehensive. Something lingered in the air, a cold sense of . . . evil!

She went to the table and lit the little lamp and returned to the door which was still open and glancing down she saw a key, Colin's key! As she bent to pick it up, her fingers touched something sticky and she dropped it in disgust. The lamplight fell upon her hand, and she saw the smear of blood!

For a long moment she stood staring, while the evil seemed to wrap around her squeezing out her life! Colin had once told her something about *obeah*, a white cock's head . . . blood smeared on a door . . . whispered incantations!

The lamp's light quivered and she realised her hand

was shaking. Moving stiffly, she went to the water-jug and carefully washed. Then she took the towel and forced herself to wipe up the stain on the floor and the trickle of blood on the door. She washed the key, working automatically and refusing to let panic swamp her, giving herself time to recover from her shock. She locked the front door and returned to bed, but kept the lamp burning beside her. Its yellow rays seemed to dissipate some of the shadowy horror that still lingered.

The key was Colin's. Lara had come that night and let herself in with Colin's key so that she could perform her hateful mission of revenge. Ram must have seen her leave and guessed what she had done. Perhaps she had heard him and had been too scared to retrieve the key. She must have stolen the key from Colin. Was he even now in a drunken sleep in some hovel where they met?

Sleep evaded her and at the first dawning light she rose. Should she tell Colin of Lara's visit? She and Colin hardly talked to each other now, and she shrank from mentioning the girl's name. If he spoke of last night and asked about his key, she would tell him, but not otherwise.

The day was unusually hot and steamy with no breeze to move the fronds of the palm trees, and for once the noisy keskidees were silent. When Melia brought the coffee, Triona remarked on the oppressive atmosphere.

'I doesn't like it, ma'am,' the cook asserted, glancing uneasily at the window. 'It seem too quiet. I think maybe a storm comes.' She waddled from the room, muttering to herself.

A storm would clear the air of the hot, faintly threatening stillness. There was no sign of Ram, and Colin, too, had not appeared, for which she was grateful. It was not the first time he had been away all night.

Last night had shaken her and she needed time to rid herself of fears and suspicions.

The heat seemed to increase and grow dense and heavy like an invisible fog. It was impossible to concentrate or settle to anything. Triona noticed the washing was not hung out and, when questioned, Melia said the washer-woman had not come that morning.

'Why, is she sick?' Triona asked, irritated. Her nerves were strung up and she felt unreasonably annoyed at the washer-woman's non-arrival.

'She not so sick,' Melia looked away. 'Maybe she don't like the storm that coming.'

'I wish it would come and end this horrid weather,' Triona said, and wandered, restless and uneasy, back to the sitting-room.

She was trying to read one of the papers Colin had ordered from England when she heard the palm leaves begin to rustle, gently at first, then with increasing force. The paper she held fluttered in the wind blowing in the window and she rose, thinking gratefully of the cooling rain that would follow.

But no rain came. The wind was gathering strength and she could see the palms bending before it and blossoms torn from the *poui* tree fly past the window and, faintly alarmed, she went into the kitchen to find it empty and no sign of Melia or her cousin. She contemplated going over to their living quarters, but the rising force of the wind stopped her. A strange far-off moaning sound from the east increased her nervousness and she hastened to let down all the shutters in the house. Even as she did so, she heard a palm fall and crash to the ground, and the next moment the house rocked slightly.

Now the storm was taking hold. Trees were lashing against each other and a crashing splintering sound followed by frenzied squawking told her the chicken-house had gone. The low moaning sound was coming nearer and merging slowly into a horrifying roar, as though the giant of fairy-tales was approaching to wreak vengeance! Again she felt the house shake, betrayed by its cheap construction and long neglect. What should she do? Where could she go? The servants' huts would not long survive this ravaging wind roaring in from the sea. She had known storms before, but never such a one as this, never a wind that sought to destroy all before it!

The roar rose to a scream and the house rocked, throwing her to the floor. Terrified, she shrank against a wall as one of the shutters was torn off and sent crashing into the trees. She was deafened by noise, rigid with primitive fear as she waited.

Abruptly there came a lull, as if the giant had paused to gather fresh strength. She heard a door crash open and the next minute a man's hands were pulling her to her feet. She looked up into Duncan's eyes.

'Quick, the house may not last.' He was urging her to the door. His voice, harsh and taut, brought her out of her dazed stupor.

'I—I can't leave . . .'

'My God, you will. This building may not stand long if the winds gets up again.'

'I—I'll be all right.'

'You'll be dead! God, woman, don't you know it's a hurricane?'

While she hesitated, he bent and picked her up and carried her from the house to where a frightened horse was straining at his rope. Then she was flung up on the saddle and clinging to him as the horse plunged forward.

The ride was a nightmare of winds screaming around them, trees bending before them and the horse's terrified shying at flying branches torn from bushes. Her hair, loosened from the net, blew across her face so that she could see nothing. Then came another pause in the storm's fury and she felt Duncan lift her down from the horse.

'I won't risk the house,' he had to shout above the wind's moaning. 'The sugar-mill is stone, we'll be safe there.'

She went with him, stunned and shivering, clinging to his arm, lost in this world of sudden chaos, her only coherent thought: *'Thank God he came for me!'*

It was dark inside the squat stone building. Duncan said, 'Stay where you are, there's a lamp somewhere.'

She heard him moving about, then there came a flare of light and she saw his torn shirt and the trickle of blood down one cheek.

'You are hurt!' she cried.

'It's nothing, a flying shingle caught me. Are you injured?' He held the lamp high, his eyes on her white face and tangle of vivid hair and her small bare feet. She had lost her slippers in that wild ride.

'No,' she said quickly. 'Only frightened. I did not realise it was a hurricane, it came so abruptly. The servants have all left.'

'They knew what was coming. I haven't a single worker here. God knows where they've gone; probably into the forest, which isn't too safe. Sit down on that bench. I've got some rum here, I think we both need it.'

She accepted it gratefully and felt her strained nerves relax somewhat and some of her composure return.

'Did you know the hurricane was coming?' she asked.

'I thought I recognised some of the signs. I'm hoping it may not last long. It is possible it is the tail-end of a storm that struck further north and is blowing itself out. I would have come for you earlier, but the wind came sooner than I expected. I've brought some things in here, rugs, a pillow and food. We'll be here for the night.'

Her hands, which were trying to smooth her hair, were stilled.

'But—I cannot stay here!'

He seated himself beside her. 'And what, pray, do you propose to do, Mrs Brooks?' There was grim amusement in his voice. 'Return on foot to your house and in bare feet? I hardly think you would get far, you know. If you are thinking of the proprieties, they have been blown away. To survive is the highest priority in a hurricane. Now finish up that rum while I see where I can house my frightened horse.'

Left alone, she looked round her at the big wooden rollers, heavy pans for the syrup and the iron implements hanging on the wall. The thick sweet smell of sugar was everywhere and dried residue dust had sifted over the floor. A coal-pot stood near with some tins, a jar of water and a kettle.

Duncan returned, the rising wind crashing the door shut behind him. He said sharply, 'Do you know where your husband is?'

'I—Well, no. He did not come home last night.' She bit her lip, wondering how much he knew. She said wearily, 'Colin has not—not been himself since learning of his father's death.'

'Since his allowance from England has ceased. Don't pretend to me, Triona. This island spells ruin for a man like your husband. He should never have come.'

'There was no alternative,' she said tightly. 'We had to leave England, and this was the only place we could come to. If we can make the estate pay . . .'

'How can it pay when the owner refuses to work it as he should? When he refuses to put his heart into it and allows his wife to shoulder all the burdens?' A sudden

crash from outside made her gasp, and he caught both
her hands in his. 'That will be one of the outhouse roofs.
This roof is strong; you are safe here.' His voice took on
a sterner note. 'But you are not safe with a man who is
drinking himself into his grave, who cares nothing for
your happiness and who . . .'

'Stop!' She tried to drag her hands away. 'Stop, I will
not listen to you!'

'. . . and who is unfaithful to you.'

She felt her anger drain away at what she saw in his
face.

'You know? Was that why . . .'

'I told you to get rid of her, yes. The girl is bad, the
servants are frightened of her and say she is an *obeah*-
woman.' His face relaxed into a grim smile. 'I gather she
got a taste of her own medicine last night. Someone left a
white cock's head outside her hut and the blood-mark on
her door—that is supposed to mean death.'

'Death?' she whispered. For a moment the big room
with its yellow lamplight and weird shadows started to
whirl. Then his arm was around her shaking shoulders
and she was pouring out the horrors of the night. She had
not meant to speak of it, to him of all people, but the
words came of their own volition and she could not stem
the tide. His arm tightened, and she heard him mutter,

'My God! The little devil!'

Outside, sounds were changing. The wind's scream
had dropped and a spatter of rain was becoming a deluge
drumming against the building. Water sprayed in
through the chinks of the shutters and snaked under the
door.

'We are on a slope,' Duncan said quietly. 'We can't be
flooded. It is as I thought, the tail-end of a hurricane and
may not last long.'

She leaned against him, empty of emotion and content

to feel his strength protecting her. A feeling of great security came to her; how long was it since she had felt secure?

At last he moved. 'I'm going to make coffee. There is a tin of biscuits, and a honeycomb and some bread. It's time you ate something.'

She watched him light a little fire in the coal-pot, fill the kettle, place it over the glowing charcoal and measure coffee into the coffee-pot. All his movements were quick and sure.

She was grateful for his silence, which allowed her time in which to compose herself. The events of the past hour had been so swift and chaotic that she had not taken in the whole implication of what had happened. She had been rescued by the man she wished to dislike. He had saved her from injury, perhaps death, and brought her to safety. She had found relief in speaking of Lara's evil intentions, and had taken strength from his strength, and she must be grateful to him. She *was* grateful, and as she watched him she knew her antagonism had gone as if carried away by the storm now in its death-throes.

'The wind is abating,' he said as he gave her a cup of strong black coffee. 'But it is raining harder. We'll be here for some time yet.'

'What will happen to our houses?'

'I shall probably find some of the shutters off, but the house was built well and should withstand a storm. I'm afraid Forest House may be damaged somewhat. It was always a ramshackle building—Haley refused to spend money on it.'

She realised she was hungry. They ate bread spread with honey and sweet biscuits, and she felt her strength return. When they had finished the meal she said abruptly, her eyes on the flickering lamp-flame, 'You came for me because you knew the house was unsafe and I was alone. I am very grateful to you for what you have done, indeed I truly do not know how to thank you. You took a great risk riding over to Forest House.'

He was at the door, plugging the gap underneath with cotton waste. He turned to her. His face was in shadow and she could not see his expression but her heart gave a leap as she heard him say slowly and strongly, 'There was nothing on earth or in hell that would have kept me from you!'

'Please . . .' she whispered, feeling her throat constrict.

'You know what I am going to say, Triona, and you cannot stop me! From the day I saw you in London you have haunted me. I tried to thrust you from me but you would not go. When we met on the boat, I knew you would never leave me as long as I lived. You have become part of me. I did not want it! I resented you . . . I think at times I hated you, as you have hated me!'

'Oh, no, I never hated you! I thought you harsh and unfriendly.'

'Because I had to fight to hide what I felt for you! Good heavens, when I thought of you tied to that weak stripling . . .'

She sprang to her feet. 'No! I am married to him!'

'Do you still love him, Triona?' He came to her in two swift strides and caught her by her shoulders. 'Can a woman such as you have any soft feelings, any loyalty, to a man who has treated you as he has?'

'Yes, I am loyal to him; he is my husband. You must say no more. I refuse to listen to you!'

'Does your heart refuse, Triona?' His eyes burned her. 'Did you dislike me because you did not wish to like me? You are beautiful, a woman of flame! You have never known love, love such as I can give you! You were

meant to be mine, Triona, and by heaven, I mean to
have you!'

She was in his arms, crushed against his body, feeling
the beat of his heart against hers! His arms imprisoned
her helplessly. His kiss, fierce, demanding, passionate,
seemed to drain her of all strength. She ceased to
struggle as fire crept through her body and she knew he
had spoken the truth! She had resented him because she
had been afraid of him! Afraid instinctively of this
terrible surge of excitement, this answering passion he
was arousing in her! His hand touched her breast and she
shivered . . .

Then her arms were round him and she was clinging to
him and returning his kisses with a passion as great as
his. Past and future were merged into this present of
blazing joy! This surge of white-hot ecstasy such as she
had never known or dreamed of.

'Master!' It was a cry from outside. Both heard it, and
Duncan raised his head. 'Master, it is Ram. I come from
the town to tell you.'

Slowly, reluctantly, Duncan's arms released her and
he turned and opened the door. In the grey light Triona
saw the small shivering figure of Ram. Water dripped
from his thin garments and one arm was wrapped in a
blood-stained piece of cloth.

'Ram! What in hell . . .'

'I come to tell you, master.' He had not seen Triona in
the shadows behind Duncan. 'The storm very bad in
town, many huts blow down. A big wave wash away
boats and jetty. The storm is going, but much damage
done. Cunha rum ship is smash down. The people run
out when it start to shake, but Mr Brooks stay inside, he
too drunk to move! The girl Lara go to pull him out,
but the roof come down and she broken up and quite
dead!'

'God!' Duncan's face tightened. 'What happened to Mr Brooks?'

Ram spread his hands. 'He dead too, master.'

CHAPTER
TEN

THE DRY season was coming to an end. Already great
banks of grey cloud were visiting the island to drench the
fields and forests that had suffered the hurricane's
onslaught.

Triona, slim and pale in her widow's weeds, sat in the
window of Norah Grantley's sitting-room looking out at
the garden where sunlight blazed down on the recently
soaked trees and bushes.

Colin was dead. The horror of the hurricane had
ended in the greatest horror of all. Her mind, numbed by
shock, had at first mercifully been deadened, but now
pictures came to torment her and she saw Colin, young,
gay and loving, her handsome husband with whom she
had shared the carefree life in London. She thought of
the love that had blossomed between them when they
first met, a love they had so confidently expected to
endure for ever.

But memory was cruel and brought another Colin
before her, ashamed and frightened when discovered,
sullen and bitter and raging uselessly against the fate of
his own making.

Her memories of events after Ram had come with the
news of Colin's death were blurred. The ride with
Duncan through the blinding rain, Norah's warm and
loving sympathy, the vicar's kindly condolences—and
tactful avoidance of the circumstances of Colin's death.

Arrangements for the funeral were made swiftly, as always in tropical climates. Triona in her black dress and veil, sitting between Norah and Mrs Fisher, had heard the service and seen the pitying glances as in a dream. Nothing had been real to her, the broken windows in the little church, the débris-strewn graveyard and crushed gardens. Only when she had returned to Norah's house did the deadening sense of unreality leave her, and she wept long and bitterly. Norah let her weep, knowing it would bring relief.

Now, sitting forlornly by the window, she was mercilessly caught in the grip of remorse and guilt. She was to blame. Colin had gone into the town because the knowledge that he had lost her love had driven him there. She had not been able to love him, but she should have tried harder to stop his drinking and to make him take a greater interest in the estate. Oh, why had she been so weak and disloyal!

Disloyal! The word was like a stab in her heart. She sprang up and began to pace to and fro feverishly as she remembered the night of the hurricane. While she had been in Duncan's arms, returning his kisses with passion as fierce as his and rejoicing in his arms around her crushing her body to his, Colin had been lying, life smashed out of his young body, in the ruins of the little rum shop, together with the girl who had tried to save him. If she could only forget that night—but it would be with her for ever.

She had been mad! Some fever in her blood had made her respond to Duncan's passion. She would forget it. She *must* forget it! But would the memory ever die? In those moments of ecstasy there had been a primitive desire to give herself to the man she had tried to hate. She had wanted him as a lover—as he had wanted her! She trembled as she recalled those moments in Duncan's arms. If Ram had not come . . .

'It is over,' she whispered, clenching her hands. 'I shall return to England and never see him again.'

Damage to the island had been sporadic. In some districts trees had been uprooted, cane flattened and huts smashed. Other places had escaped all but minor harm. The wave that had wrecked boats in Carib harbour had washed away the town's two jetties, but the hill above the town, where the big houses lay, had escaped the full force of the storm as it pursued its twisting course across the island.

One evening Norah asked Triona about her plans for the future.

'I shall return to England,' Triona said. 'But of course I shall have to sell the estate first.'

Norah looked thoughtful. 'I'm afraid that may not be easy, especially after the damage the storm has done. You will need help, and the best person to give it is Duncan Ross.'

'Oh no!' Triona turned her head to avoid her friend's surprised glance.

'Why not? What have you against him?'

'I simply do not wish to accept help from him, that is all.'

Norah was a kindly woman but she could speak plainly when she wished to. Her expression changed somewhat as she said, 'Triona, you have had time to recover a little from the shock of your husband's death. I know you truly grieved, although he wasn't . . . Well, it is time you took hold of your emotions and behaved sensibly.'

Triona swung around to stare. 'My emotions? I am not aware . . .'

'No, you aren't, which is why I'm going to be unkind and tell you that you are behaving in a neurotic and unstable manner. Colin's death was tragic, but inevitable, I think. I suspect you are blaming yourself for much of his unfortunate behaviour and drowning yourself in guilt in a most unwise and unhealthy way. You feel you could have saved him from destroying himself. Well, you are wrong, and when you cease your self-mortification you will realise this.'

'It is not true!' Triona cried, stung.

'It is. You are indulging in useless regrets instead of facing facts honestly. You are not weak, my dear. You have suffered more than most women, and it has not broken you. You must be strong now.'

Triona looked away. Norah's words hurt, but she knew they were true. The Colin she had loved was not the same Colin who now lay in the little churchyard and for whom she could feel pity, but no more.

Norah's voice brought her out of her troubled thoughts.

'Have you quite forgotten that Duncan risked injury to rescue you from your home in the hurricane?'

'No, of course not,' she said through stiff lips. 'I shall always be grateful to him. But . . .'

'But you are too proud to accept help from him. Now be sensible, Triona. Duncan has already set some of his men to repairing the roof of Forest House, you have that to thank him for as well. He has something to put before you, and you will be most unwise if you don't consider it, and take his advice. I've asked him to come tomorrow so that you can talk to him.'

Triona was silent. To meet Duncan, the man for whom for a wild moment she had felt such a fierce, deep longing, appalled her. Although it must have been a momentary madness born of her unhappiness and loneliness, *he* would put a wrong construction on her behaviour. He would think she loved him!

Slowly her agitation subsided and she realised she could not hope to avoid him. She owed him much. He had saved her in the storm and now he was repairing her home. She would have to meet him, but she would make her feelings clear to him. His friendship would be welcome, but nothing more. Would he accept friendship? She thrust away memories of his words declaring his love for her, a love he had striven to hide.

She slept badly that night and there were dark shadows under her eyes next morning, and the dread of what she must face was still with her.

Norah had gone into the town, and Triona was alone in the sitting-room when the maid showed Duncan in. She sat pale but composed in her black gown with its tiny frill of white at throat and wrist, the bright sunlight turning her hair to glowing flame. Her eyes were steady as she raised them to his, but she could feel the quickened beat of her heart shaking her body.

'You are pale and thin,' he said abruptly. 'Are you well?'

'Quite well, thank you. Norah has been all that is kind and good to me.'

He nodded. 'Yes, she has a great heart.'

He, too, looked thinner and there were signs of strain in his face. The strong line of his jaw was more pronounced and his eyes, deep-set under heavy brows, held a sombre light.

She kept her head high under his intent scrutiny, determined he should not know how strongly his personality affected her or how dismayingly she was aware of him. 'Please tell me what damage my house has suffered.'

He started, as though his thoughts had been elsewhere. 'The roof is damaged and the servants' quarters wrecked. I'm afraid rain has damaged furniture and you will have to replace some things.'

'Not if I sell the estate,' she said quickly.

He was silent for a moment, frowning. 'You have decided to sell?'

Confidence was returning to her and, with it, composure. His manner was matter of fact and held no hint of the ardour she feared. He respected her situation, the newly bereft young widow. He claimed no intimacy, betrayed no memory of the night of the hurricane. She need not have imagined the meeting would be embarrassing.

She spread her hands. 'How can I manage an estate on my own? Will it be possible to sell it soon?'

He shrugged. 'At a price, perhaps. Do you mean to return to England?'

'Yes.' She avoided his searching eye. 'There is nothing to keep me here.'

'How will you manage there? Your husband told me something of your circumstances. You have no relations except for an elderly aunt who could not support you, and your brother-in-law.'

'I would never accept help from Edward!' she exclaimed.

'But your husband would have been prepared to.' He shook his head. 'Forgive me, I did not mean to speak of him.'

Her throat tightened. He knew Colin's weaknesses so well, that it was useless to defend them.

'Will it be easy to find a buyer for Forest?' she asked again.

'Whoever buys it will have much replanting to do. But I have several suggestions to make. First, that you should get the house in order so that you can live in it. Then that you finish building the three bungalows which

Haley started before he ran out of money. I think the
bank would give you a loan. The government staff is to
be increased and more accommodation will be needed,
and I am certain you will be able to rent the bungalows
profitably.'

'But all that will take time,' she objected uneasily.

He shook his head. 'Juan Geira takes contracts for
building. It is a paying side-line for him, and his men
work well and quickly. And he will not press for immedi-
ate payment.' A wry smile touched his lips. 'He has great
admiration for beauty.'

She was silent for some moments, her mind busy. For
the first time since Colin's death she felt a stir of interest
in the estate as she considered Duncan's suggestion.

He spoke again. 'I want to buy that part of your estate
adjoining my cane fields. I mean to increase the crop of
cane now that more markets are opening up for sugar.
No,' he caught her swift glance. 'I'm not being charit-
able; I need that land and, if you agree to sell, I'll start
clearing and planting it at once.' He rose. 'Don't decide
anything until you have thought it over and discussed it
with someone. But I think you should talk to Juan about
building your servants' quarters so that your staff can
return.'

As he turned to leave her, she put out her hand. 'Wait.
I have not thanked you for your help, for all you have
done for me. Believe me, I am deeply grateful.'

He swung around and she caught her breath when she
saw his eyes.

'I do not want your gratitude, Triona. You know well
enough what I want, but I shall not speak of it yet.'

She rose, forcing herself to meet his burning gaze.
'I—I do not wish you ever to speak of it. I am most
grateful to you, but gratitude is all I shall ever have to
offer you, please believe me.'

He took a swift step towards her and for a second she thought he would catch her in his arms. But he did not touch her. Only the slight involuntary movement of a muscle in his cheek told her of the curb he was putting on himself.

'I will not believe that.' His voice was level but something fierce lay beneath his words, making her tremble. 'I shall never believe it. I shall wait . . . but not for ever!' He left her, and she heard him calling to the house-boy to bring his horse.

Her mind was in turmoil. For him to have spoken as he had when she was still in mourning for her husband! But Duncan knew she no longer loved Colin; he had known it when she had remained willingly in his arms, returning his kisses—and now he was certain he had her love!

But she did not love him! Passion had betrayed her on the terrible night, and guilt would always make the memory a shameful one for her.

She thrust his last words from her mind. When she was less agitated, she would write to him and make her feelings clear.

She forced herself to consider calmly his suggestions about the bungalows, and selling part of the estate to him. When the Fishers called, she asked their advice. Both ideas received unqualified approval. The vicar recommended a lawyer she could trust, and urged her to settle the sale with Duncan as soon as possible.

'I do not wish to be thought interfering, Mrs Brooks,' he said. 'But I imagine the money will be useful to you in helping to pay for building the bungalows.'

'I believe there are three arrivals expected here soon,' Mrs Fisher said. 'And they will be looking for somewhere to live. Some of the houses they might have had were destroyed in the storm.'

That evening Triona wrote to Duncan. It was a difficult letter, and she had made three attempts before she was satisfied with the result. Norah's boy would deliver it to Toco next morning.

She wondered how Duncan would react. Would he come storming in, angry and resentful, accusing her of deceiving him about her true feelings? Would he reassert his love and determination to have her? She wandered about the house, uneasy and restless.

Mail came, and there was a letter from her aunt who had not received news of Colin's death. Triona found comfort in the loving words and had a longing to see the one person who truly loved her. Mrs Morton wrote of the small, familiar things of her quiet life and it sounded to Triona as though she had written from another world, a world in which she had once lived and been happy and secure. Was it possible to go back to that life? *I have changed*, she thought. *I am not not the person who left England*.

She was sitting on the veranda. An hour's heavy rain had left the garden dripping but had not eased the sultry atmosphere, and she longed for a cool breeze to lighten the steamy air. Hearing a sound, she saw a horseman riding up to the house, and she knew it was Duncan. She had a moment of panic and half rose, meaning to retreat into the house, but he had seen her, and pride made her sink back and watch him dismount and enter the veranda.

He spoke without preamble. 'I received your letter. I do not mean to discuss it, beyond saying that you need not fear I shall cause you distress. Now, have you thought over my proposition that you sell me some of your land?'

For a moment she had no words to answer him. Surprise, relief and uncertainty held her silent. Did he mean it? Was it a trick? His face told her nothing.

'Please sit down,' she murmured. 'Yes, I have thought about it and discussed it with Norah and the Fishers, and they think I would be wise to do as you suggest. I have spoken to Juan Geira, who is willing to put men to work on the bungalows at once. He awaits my final decision.'

'And you will sell me the land immediately?'

She nodded. She was still feeling bewildered. The interview was taking a different turn from what she had expected.

'I have contacted Mr Fisher's lawyer, who will handle my affairs from now on.'

'Good.' He seated himself, stretching out his long legs. 'You can trust him; he's clever and honest, not a usual combination out here. Now about the land: I would like to start clearing it as soon as possible.'

The conversation became businesslike. Triona agreed to tell Geira to start work at once. The wet season was not good for building, but that could not be helped.

Outside, trees and shrubs dripped. Clouds like a thick grey blanket pressed down on the land, promising more rain. A scrawny hen picked languidly for ants. The air had a stifling, humid heaviness that seemed to dull the senses.

Triona lay back, pushing her hair off her damp forehead. 'How I dislike this weather!'

'Without rain, we would have no crops,' he said. He was leaning back in his chair, his hands thrust in his pockets, his eyes on the garden. This was the Duncan she had so resented: cold, impatient, unaware of her. Looking at him, she could not believe he was the same man who had declared his love so fiercely and who had said, 'By heaven, I mean to have you!'

She heard Norah call out, 'Stay and have a drink, Duncan.'

He rose and went the sitting-room door. 'I must

go, Norah, I have work to do.' He turned to Triona. 'Goodbye, Mrs Brooks.'

'Please tell me, before you go,' she said quickly. 'Is Ram all right now? Has his arm healed—and what has happened to my other servants?'

'Ram is well and working on your garden. The other servants are in town and ready to return to you.'

She watched him ride away, conscious of feeling oddly dissatisfied. Because he had not appeared to resent her letter? Because he had not demanded more than the friendship she offered?

That night she did not go to bed at once but stood looking out into the darkness lit by the fireflies' pin-points of light, aware of a vexation of spirit for which she could not account. Her meeting with Duncan had been conducted on businesslike lines, as she had intended it should. He appeared to accept her stipulation that nothing but friendship was possible between them with unconcern bordering on indifference. The time before, he had said he did not believe her . . . that he would wait . . . Now it appeared he had decided to believe her after all. The sudden, oddly mortifying, thought came to her that he might have discovered that his regard for her was the obsession of a lonely man whose life had been soured by unjust suspicion, and perhaps the fact that she had been out of reach, the wife of another man, had been part of her attraction for him. If this were indeed so she was glad, she told herself firmly.

But, despite her declared gladness, she did not sleep until dawn slid through her window.

CHAPTER
ELEVEN

'BUT YES, señora, I send men to work at once.' Juan Geira shrugged his shoulders. 'It is not so good, no, to build in the wet season, but I have done such a thing before and it is possible.' He sighed as he looked at Triona in her widow's weeds. 'So young and beautiful to know so much sadness . . . Forgive me, señora, I do not wish to be impertinent.'

'I know you do not,' she said. 'I appreciate your sympathy. Tell me, please, can my servants' quarters be rebuilt soon?'

'But most certainly. They are wooden huts with palm-leaf roofs; they need no skill to build. When do you return to Forest, señora?'

'When the house is ready. I hope it will not be long.' She hesitated, before going on a little anxiously, 'I may not be able to pay you all I will owe you at once, but when the bungalows are rented.'

He raised his hand swiftly. 'Señora, please to say no more. It is of no matter when I am paid.'

'But you will have to pay for materials and pay your men.' She thought of the excellent price Duncan was to pay her for the land when the sale had finally gone through. 'I shall, of course, pay you something on account.'

'I am in no need of money. My store does well and I have other little businesses.'

She knew one of the little businesses was the liquor store he had just opened adjoining the store. He had captured Cunha's trade, although the store was run on very different lines.

Letters had arrived from Mrs Morton and Edward, in whom the news of Colin's death had aroused very different reactions. Mrs Morton wrote, deeply shocked, from a heart full of true sympathy and anxiety for Triona's future. Edward's epistle breathed pious sorrow and oblique reference to the wages of sin.

Norah was all kindness, and her friendship meant much to Triona who longed, nevertheless, to be back in her own home. No doubt it was delayed shock at the tragedy of Colin's death that was making her so restless and depressed. Perhaps the days would seem less blank and meaningless if she were at home and busy with household affairs.

Norah agreed with her. 'I'd love to keep you, my dear, but I believe the time has come when you must be on your own. You have good servants who will look after you, and I know Duncan will be there to help you.'

When at last she returned to Forest, Triona found much to be done in the house and she was kept busy. Geira had been as good as his word, and the servants' huts were ready and Melia and her cousin installed. Ram, quietly industrious as ever, had cleared away much of the débris the storm had left and was busy planting vegetables and salvaging such banana plants as had survived.

Triona visited the bungalows, on which work had started, with Ram. 'The land around will have to be cleared and planted, and there is no road.'

'There is a road,' Ram told her.' But much grows over it. It will not be too difficult to find.'

Duncan came to see the work, and suggested a few

alterations in the buildings. He told Triona he would send some men over to uncover the road Haley had built and which had been badly overgrown. His visit was short, and she did not press him to stay although honesty made her admit to herself that she would have liked to. Norah was away visiting Trinidad, and the Fishers were on leave in St Lucia, and she found the days long and lonely.

Duncan had accepted her ruling that she would never offer him more than friendship. That, surely, was what she wished? She found herself wondering if his love had died when she repulsed him, and was startled and uneasy by the bleak discontent the thought brought.

One afternoon she was busy filling some hanging baskets with ferns Ram had brought her from the forest when a smart equipage drove up and she saw with surprise that she was to be honoured by a visit from Mrs Winkworth and three strangers.

Mrs Winkworth introduced her friends. 'Mr and Mrs Ashton and Mrs Ellison are newly arrived from England and seeking somewhere to live that is not too far from Regina. I have heard, Mrs Brooks, that you will soon have a bungalow to rent. Mr and Mrs Ashton would like to view it.'

'Certainly, Mrs Winkworth.' Triona liked the look of the young couple, whose manner was open and friendly. Mrs Ellison, a startlingly beautiful brunette, was more reserved, and Triona wondered what relation she was to the Ashtons.

Mrs Winkworth provided the information by saying, 'Mrs Ellison is Mr Ashton's widowed sister. When will the bungalow be ready, Mrs Brooks?'

'I hope quite soon. The wet season has made things difficult.'

She led them down the newly cleared road and the

Ashtons expressed approval bordering on enthusiasm at the almost completed bungalow. Mrs Ellison seemed less satisfied.

'Surely it is a trifle small?' she suggested, holding up the skirt of her elegant gown so it did not touch the damp ground. 'And there is no lawn or garden.'

'I shall plant a lawn and garden,' Triona told her. 'Things grow so quickly here that you will not have long to wait.'

'I think it is perfectly charming,' Mrs Ashton declared.

'And not too far from the town,' her husband remarked. 'I suppose I must have a horse; I see no accommodation for a carriage.'

'We must have a carriage, my dear Mark,' his sister said swiftly. 'Effie and I do not intend to be kept prisoners, you know. We shall visit friends and explore the island.'

Triona was somewhat dismayed. She had not thought of a carriage-house or stables and, of course, people would need both. She heard a step behind her and turned to see Duncan.

She introduced him to the new arrivals, explaining the object of their visit. 'Unfortunately I find I have forgotten to plan for a stable and carriage-house,' she told him.

'But Juan has not forgotten,' he told her. 'He is going to suggest he builds them as soon as the house is finished.'

'Oh, that will be excellent,' Mrs Ellison murmured. Her large and lovely eyes rested on him with approval. 'Pray, do you live near here, Mr Ross?'

'My estate adjoins Forest.'

'Really?' She continued to keep her eyes upon him, a tiny smile parting her pretty lips. 'Then we shall be neighbours.'

'I look forward to that pleasure,' he said with a slight bow.

Triona glanced at him. He was wearing a white shirt open at the neck and white trousers tucked into wet-weather boots. There was, as always, an air of controlled force about him, a hint of arrogance and strong passions held back. He was not handsome, but he had a masculine virility many men would envy. She could see that the Ashtons were impressed, and Mrs Ellison was finding it difficult to take her eyes off him.

'I'm afraid it will take time to put up stables,' she told the Ashtons.

'In the meantime, would it not be possible for Mr Ashton to use the stables at Forest House?' Duncan suggested.

'Oh, of course,' Triona exclaimed. The sooner she could rent the bungalow, the sooner she could pay Juan. 'There is plenty of room, and you are welcome to use it.'

She took her visitors back to the house, and the maid brought tea. Mrs Ashton was full of questions about servants, shopping and the social life of the island, while her husband entertained Mrs Winkworth with news of England.

Mrs Ellison had drawn Duncan to the window and was conducting a sprightly conversation with him. She was obviously aware of her beauty and ability to charm the other sex. Triona, glancing at her from time to time, thought she did not care much for her and hoped her visit to her brother would not be over-long.

The party departed after the Ashtons had said they definitely wished to have the bungalow as soon as possible. Mrs Ellison took a somewhat protracted farewell of Duncan, demanding with pretty assurance that he promise to show her some of the beauties of Ste-Martine.

'It is not at its best in the wet season,' he told her.

'Oh, I am content to wait,' she answered, smiling up at him. 'Everything is so deliciously different from England. You know, I wondered if I should enjoy visiting the island much, but now,' she dropped her eyes, letting her silky lashes brush her cheeks, 'I am *certain* I shall.'

Triona waited until the carriage was out of sight before turning to Duncan to say, 'It seems I am to have neighbours quite soon. The Ashtons appear to be charming people, don't you think?'

He nodded, and she sensed his mind was elsewhere. With the lovely Mrs Ellison? It was odd how unpleasant she found the idea.

'Have you had any offers for the estate?' he asked abruptly.

'No. The lawyer says it will not be easy to sell it.'

'I'm afraid he is right. In the meantime you are not badly situated. You will soon have more tenants.' He frowned as he looked at her. 'You are looking tired. Are you well?'

'Oh yes, I am quite well, thank you,' she said, feeling a tiny glow of pleasure at his concern. 'I do find this weather somewhat trying, I fear.'

'We all do. But it won't last much longer. I must go. Let me know if there is anything I can do, or if you get an offer for the estate.'

When he had left, she knew she would have liked him to stay. She was relying on his strength and help these days. Nothing in his manner gave any hint of those feelings that had so shaken and disturbed her on the night of the hurricane.

Mrs Morton wrote, pressing her niece to return to England, and Triona was finding it difficult to answer. Her aunt knew nothing of Colin's behaviour or the failure of their marriage. She had not written of the problems that now faced her and the difficulty of finding a buyer for the estate.

She was missing Norah sorely. Sometimes a nervous energy seized her and she would work in the house or garden or drive into town. At other times a curious lethargy enveloped her and she would sit watching the storm-clouds pour their store of rain upon the land. At night she often lay listening to the chorus of frogs and cicadas, her thoughts uneasy and fearful. What lay in the future if she could not sell the estate? She must have money to return to England, and, when she got there, how would she live? Her aunt would willingly give her a home, but her tiny income could not support them both. She would have to find work . . .

The rains slowly decreased in force and the first bungalow was at last finished and the ground cleared and planted. The Ashtons decided to move in, and Triona, glad of something to keep uneasy thoughts at bay, helped them.

She found the young couple friendly and lively, but her first, unfavourable, impression of Mrs Flora Ellison had deepened into active dislike. The lovely widow soon showed where her interest lay, and Triona was startled to see how often Duncan's horse was tethered outside the bungalow. It would seem that he found the lady's company attractive.

After a visit to the lawyer one day, Triona sent a note by the house-boy asking Duncan to call and give her his opinion on the offer of a planter from St Lucia. When she heard his step she put down her sewing and, meeting his eyes, she was swept with a feeling of deep pleasure and said impulsively, 'You do not not call often now.'

He seated himself beside her. 'I was not aware you wished me to.'

'But of course I am always pleased to see you. I much appreciate all the help you have given me. But perhaps . . .' she could not help saying it, 'you do not have so much time now the Ashtons have come and are proving such charming neighbours.'

'They are certainly very pleasant people,' he said calmly. 'I think you are lucky to have them living near; they will be good friends.'

'I hope so.' When he said no more, she added, 'I suppose Mrs Ellison will be returning to England soon.'

'Not yet. She tells me she is enchanted with Ste-Martine and has decided to stay longer. Now, tell me about this offer you have had.'

When she told him, he advised her not to accept, saying it was too low and that she should wait for something better.

As he rose to leave her, she had an impulse to ask his opinion of Flora Ellison. Did he find her attractive? Duncan had little use for social dalliance, but a beautiful, beguiling woman who displayed such strong liking for his company might lure him from his seclusion.

Her thoughts were interrupted by his asking suddenly, 'Must you continue to wear black? It does not suit you and makes you look pale.'

She sighed. 'I admit I dislike it. It is not really suitable for a tropical climate, but convention . . .'

'To the devil with convention! It is time you were done with grieving, Triona.' She was taken aback by the harsh note in his voice. 'Colin's death was a tragedy, but it did not mean heartbreak for you. He brought you great unhappiness and pain. He told me something of the reason why he had to come out to Ste-Martine.'

'No, he would never have told you that!' she cried in distress.

'You could say it was the rum talking,' he said dryly.

'It is no business of mine to condemn him for it. But to make *you* suffer . . . For that I do not forgive him.'

She raised her hand. 'Please do not speak of it. All that is past and I do not wish to remember it. We were happy once.'

'But you have had little happiness here,' he insisted, cruelly, she thought. 'He killed your love, you cannot deny it. It was not possible for you to care for the man he became. You were loyal, you were silent about your sufferings, but there were few people who were not aware of the inherent weakness that was destroying him.'

She looked away from his searching gaze as she said, 'I was his wife.'

'Triona . . .' he began. Suddenly he put out his hand and touched the burnished glory of her hair, and she heard him say beneath his breath, 'Lady of Flame . . . and ice!' before he turned on his heel and strode from the room.

She stood by the window watching him ride off. How well she knew the set of his broad shoulders and the quick turn of his head when something caught his attention. She sighed as she turned away. Of course she had been right to make her feelings plain to him, yet an innate honesty told her she had been piqued by his easy acceptance of her offer of friendship.

That stormy night of the hurricane meant nothing to him now. Duncan was a man of ardent nature long repressed, a lonely man with a tragedy dogging him. The circumstances of that night, the fury and excitement of the storm, being alone with a young and beautiful woman whom he had rescued, had aroused a madness in him which no doubt he was now regretting.

Madness. Yes, it had been that. It had been a madness which had stirred her blood so strangely. The moments of ecstasy in his arms, her joyous abandonment to his hungry kisses, had been something as primitive and overwhelming as the storm.

She put her hands to her burning cheeks. That night must be forgotten, be buried for ever. Duncan had accepted her friendship; was that not what she wanted? He felt pity for her, his anger against Colin proved that. But he was dangerous, she knew that now, and it would be wise to avoid seeing him. He had helped her in many ways, but she would not seek his advice again.

It was some days later when she saw the Ashton carriage drive up to the house. Mrs Ashton had come with an invitation.

'Now that the weather is better, we are planning to visit the west coast of the island next Sunday and we shall be so pleased, dear Mrs Brooks, if you will consent to join us. Flora is quite determined to see all the beauty spots while she is with us. I believe the west coast is very fine, and the drive through parts of the forest will be most interesting. Do say you will come!'

Triona accepted with pleasure. Here was something to occupy her and keep uneasy thoughts at bay.

The day dawned fine. Colours were brilliant and fresh after the rain, and a quick breeze was singing through the palms. She wished she need not wear her black dress, but social convention decreed deep mourning for the husband she could not mourn. She chose a wide cream straw hat and felt a little lift in her spirits when she looked in her glass. She was still too thin and she had not regained her fresh colour, but she was looking better than she had since Colin's death. She caught up her parasol and ran out of the house as the Ashton carriage drove up.

Mark Ashton helped her into the carriage. He still had

the pink and white complexion of a new arrival and his lively manner pleased her. His wife, charming in what was obviously a trousseau dress of pink linen, smiled as she made room for Triona beside her.

'What a delightful little island this is, Mrs Brooks. Mark and I wondered if we would like living here, as it *is* rather off the map, isn't it? Have you visited the other side of the island yet?'

Triona confessed she had not. She was enjoying the ride in the comfortable little carriage and lively conversation with her companions. Mrs Ellison, elegant in misty blue silk, a gown rather too elaborate for the occasion, had given her a polite smile and turned her attention to the road ahead. Suddenly she cried,

'There he is! How well he sits his horse.'

Triona looked up and was astonished to see Duncan riding towards them. She exclaimed, 'I did not know Mr Ross was to accompany us.'

Flora Ellison laughed knowingly. 'Oh, he said he must work, but I persuaded him it was wrong to work on a Sunday. Indeed, I quite insisted.'

'You must have been persuasive indeed,' her brother remarked. 'From what I hear, Ross is not much given to appearing in company.'

'Perhaps it depends on the company,' his sister murmured sweetly and flashed a brilliant smile at Duncan as he rode up.

Triona was silent, aware of a mixture of emotions that bade fair to spoil her enjoyment. Flora Ellison was an accomplished flirt and used to using her charm unstintedly on men. She was using this charm on Duncan now, possibly because he was the only man at hand at the moment. Did Duncan recognise this and was he merely amusing himself by letting her flirt with him, Triona wondered unhappily, or was he seriously in danger of mistaking a coquette's desire for another victim for a deeper feeling, and responding to it?

He rode beside the carriage, next to Flora who had summoned him. His eyes went to Triona, and he drew back to say, 'You are still wearing black.'

Flora caught his words. 'Black in this climate is vastly unbecoming. After my period of mourning I wore lavender and shades of purple, something which I fear Mrs Brooks unfortunately cannot do with her shade of hair. I am lucky to be able to look well in all colours.'

They had made an early start, and the vivid green of bamboo, palm and mango tree delighted the eye as they drove at a smart pace down a dirt road. Keskidees fluttered through the trees and once an agouti, a hare-like animal much prized for its flesh, darted across their path.

The forest grew thicker until it became jungle, and here the great trees reared above them, their trunks festooned with trailing creepers. A pungent, steamy smell came from the undergrowth and, as the trees closed overhead, Triona had the eerie sensation of being enclosed in a great green cage. Strange and beautiful flowers caught her eye. Sometimes there came a break in the lush growth around them allowing a glimpse of a hill ribbed by many rainfalls.

'Oh, an orchid!' Flora leaned forward, pointing excitedly. 'Stop, boy,' she ordered the negro groom. 'Duncan, I *must* have it! And there are more further in the forest. I can have a bouquet of them! Pick them for me, won't you, please?' She turned her fine dark eyes pleadingly on Duncan.

Triona said sharply, 'It is dangerous to walk in the jungle; there are snakes. The fer-de-lance and coral snakes are deadly.'

Flora ignored her. She pouted prettily. 'You are

wearing boots, Mr Ross, you will not be bitten. I simply must have those orchids.'

'They won't last,' Triona protested. 'They will be dead before we reach the coast.'

'Yes, Flora, you're wasting time,' her brother told her. 'Drive on, boy.'

'Mr Ross!' Flora looked at him imploringly, but he shook his head.

'Mrs Brooks is right, they will die. I shall send one of my boys into the forest to get you a plant, and you can keep it in your garden on a tree. It will grow on any piece of wood.'

Flora sank back in her seat and for a second her mouth tightened unpleasantly. Then she smiled at him. '*How* kind of you, Mr Ross. Of course I would rather have a plant. It was so thoughtful of you to think of it.'

The journey proceeded with little Mrs Ashton exclaiming at every new vista. Flora sat, apparently absorbed in the scenery, but Triona saw how often her eyes turned to Duncan riding easily beside her. Triona was still surprised that he had consented to come with them. Was it because of Flora? The thought brought a strange and unhappy pang to her heart. She tried to convince herself that, since Duncan was now a good and helpful friend, it was natural she did not wish to see him the plaything of a heartless flirt, but that did not completely account for the flash of anger she had felt for Flora when she ordered Duncan to get her the orchid as if he were her devoted slave. Duncan would be no woman's slave—he would be master.

The road left the jungle and came to a wide stretch of coastland. At Duncan's direction, they made for a promontory from where the ground sloped down gently to a grove of palms on the edge of a beach.

'There will be shade,' he explained, 'and a breeze.'

They left the carriage and followed the groom bearing the luncheon basket down to the beach. Triona paused in delight to watch the aquamarine sea, shadowed with purple where reefs lay beneath, curling up on to the white coral sand and breaking with a hiss into silvery froth.

'Oh, how lovely,' she breathed, her blue eyes shining. The wind fluttered the skirts of her thin dress and teased a strand of vivid hair from under her hat. Suddenly she was conscious of Duncan beside her.

'I'm glad you came today,' he said quietly. 'You need to go about more.'

'Oh yes, I do agree,' Flora's voice made Triona turn her head. 'But unfortunately Mrs Brooks's recent tragic bereavement must prevent her from appearing in society for some time if she is not to arouse unkind criticism.' She sighed. 'Social laws are indeed hard on us poor women, I fear.'

Triona walked away. She disliked and distrusted Flora Ellison, but it would be unwise to allow it to become apparent. She rejoined the Ashtons and helped to unpack the luncheon basket.

'Where has Flora got to?' Mrs Ashton asked suddenly. 'We should have luncheon before it gets too hot.'

Her husband shaded his eyes with his hand as he looked along the beach. 'She has gone off with Ross. I expect she will make him collect shells for her. Flora is a magpie, you know.' He turned to smile at Triona, who had removed her hat to let the sea breeze cool her hot face . 'She has to collect things, even when she has no use for them.'

Triona looked at the distant figures. Flora collected compliments, admiration and men. Would she collect Duncan Ross?

They returned, Flora with a handful of shells. 'There

are so few,' she complained. 'We do better on an English beach.'

Lunch was pleasant in the shade of the tall coconut palms. The groom had brought rugs and cushions from the carriage and, after they had eaten, the women lay drowsing, lulled by the monotonous surge and fall of the sea, while the two men set off to walk to a further bay.

Mrs Ashton slept peacefully, and Triona was gently dozing when she heard Flora move closer and murmur, 'Dear Mrs Brooks, I do most truly feel for you in the distress and unhappiness you have had to suffer. Mr Ross has told me . . .'

Triona sat up abruptly, her eyes wide with shock. 'I do not believe he told you anything!'

'Oh, pray do not imagine I would breathe a *word*. I am silent as the grave about what is confided in me. How you must long to leave this island. You know, I do agree with Mr Ross that it would be best if you returned to England as soon as possible.'

Triona was shocked into silence. Was it possible that Duncan had discussed her with this woman? She felt instinctively that Flora was not trustworthy, yet she obviously knew of Colin's ruin and the failure of their marriage. She had an abrupt, bleak sense of isolation, of betrayal. So Duncan thought—perhaps wished—she should leave Ste-Martine as soon as possible. He had never said so, but he had thought it and expressed the thought to Flora.

The day was ruined for her. She pleaded a headache to account for her silence on the drive back. The Ashtons were sympathetic, and Effie offered eau de cologne and suggested a rest as soon as she reached Forest House.

As she left the carriage, Duncan dismounted and strode over to her. 'You look unwell. Let me . . .'

'I shall go and lie down directly,' she said quickly, not

looking at him. 'I shall be quite all right when I have rested.'

She thanked the Ashtons and went swiftly into the house. Her head was truly aching now and weariness weighted her limbs. She told herself that for once the heat had affected her, but Flora's words kept returning to her as she lay in the darkened room, 'I do agree with Mr Ross that it would be best if you returned to England as soon as possible.'

CHAPTER
TWELVE

MELIA PLACED the dish of chicken curry before Triona and stood back, her hands folded in her apron.

'Mistress Grantley cook say she mistress come back yesterday.'

Triona looked up quickly. 'Yesterday? I thought she meant to remain away longer.'

'She cook say she come back.'

'Oh, I'm so pleased,' Triona said happily.

'Yes, ma'am. Mistress Grantley is a nice nice lady. She order she carriage for this afternoon so's she can visit with you.'

'Did her cook tell you all this, Melia?'

'True, ma'am. I see she las' night at the funeral.'

'Oh dear, whose funeral was it?'

'Well, I doesn't rightly know, ma'am, but it was a nice nice funeral.' Melia bobbed a curtsy and departed.

The news of her friend's return filled Triona with pleasure, and she was waiting impatiently at the window when the Grantley carriage drove up.

'Oh, how glad I am to see you, Norah!' Triona kissed her visitor warmly. 'You don't know how I have missed you. Come and tell me all about your visit to Trinidad. I did not realise you intended to return so soon.'

'I did not intend to, but something I learned there has brought me back.'

'Oh?' Triona looked more closely at her friend and

saw her face was unusually grave. 'Is it something serious, Norah?'

'It is serious enough for me to return to warn Duncan.'

'*Warn* him?' Triona caught her breath. 'I don't understand. What threatens him?'

'I am not certain, but I think trouble may lie ahead for him. I found out that Felix Craig is in Port of Spain.'

Triona looked bewildered. 'Who is Felix Craig?'

'Angela Ross's brother, Duncan's brother-in-law. He did his best at the inquest to have Duncan accused, and swore he would never give up his search for evidence that Duncan was guilty of his sister's murder. He is a weak, vicious man, but I think he loved his sister. Already there is talk of bringing Duncan to Trinidad to stand trial. Felix Craig has declared that he has evidence that Duncan's servants lied about the night of the murder, and that Duncan did not go fishing.'

'But surely no one would accept such evidence now?' Triona protested. 'Servants are notoriously unreliable. They forget, and they can imagine things.'

'Well, it's in my mind that Felix Craig has probably bribed the boys. It is quite likely they have forgotten what actually happened that night but are ready to be paid for lying about it. If Craig calls for a trial, he may well get it, I fear. He has some sort of government position and can pull strings—and he is wealthy.'

'But Duncan was not accused,' Triona cried. 'He cannot be tried now!'

'My dear, the laws out here are not the same as laws in England in some ways,' Norah sighed. 'I would not like to say there is corruption, but . . .'

'There were other men,' Triona burst out. 'She had lovers, probably many. The American man may have discovered what manner of woman she was . . . Or that Spanish boy. Spaniards are hot-headed and passionate;

he may have been discarded in favour of a wealthier lover and taken his revenge. What happened to him?'

'I believe it was established that he had left the island. It was generally known that Manuel Casulla was Angela's lover for a time. There was no evidence against him, although he was the one I would have suspected.'

'What about the American man?'

'He was in Caracas; she had planned to meet him there. Give me some tea, my dear, I am in sore need of it. I must see Duncan when I leave you. I'm praying it may be a false alarm, but he had better know what is brewing in Port of Spain and that he has a clever and vicious enemy in Felix Craig.'

When she was alone, Triona sprang up, unable to sit still, her mind full of what Norah had told her. In spite of all she knew of Duncan, the reserve that hid an iron will and passionate nature, she was convinced he was innocent. And now he might be dragged through the agony of re-opened wounds to prove it. Why had Felix Craig waited so long? Had he been plotting and planning these last four years, his mind twisted by his obsession of Duncan's guilt?

Norah was right, she thought. Craig had bribed Duncan's servants. But their evidence would break down when they were questioned in court and became frightened, and Craig's unscrupulous character would be revealed.

She tried to keep her thoughts turned away from what Norah had discovered in Trinidad, but it was not possible, and the next day she could no longer bear the uncertainty, ordered the carriage and drove into town. Norah was at home.

'I had to come,' Triona said abruptly 'I had to know if Duncan had heard anything.'

Norah was looking pale and worried. 'He has heard nothing. Whether he is worried or not I wouldn't know; Duncan does not reveal his feelings.'

'But he was never accused,' Triona said desperately. 'They cannot charge him after all this time!'

'The finding was an open one by Trinidad law,' Norah said, and rang the bell on a table beside her. 'I'm having a drink, and so are you. I think we both need it. Now let us talk of something else, my dear. After all, we may be upsetting ourselves about something that will not happen. Mrs Ashton called before I went away. She's a pretty little thing, and lively, but her handsome sister-in-law looked bored with our conversation and brightened up only when that young police officer dropped in.' Norah sniffed disparagingly. 'She's not what I call a *comfortable* person. By the way, I heard that Geira has in a consignment of English biscuits. You'd best hurry if you want some.'

Triona remembered her friend's advice on the way through the town, and stopped to order biscuits and some groceries in the Spaniard's store. 'And some laundry soap,' she added.

'But certainly, I will parcel the goods for you.' He dropped the packet of soap, and she noticed his hands were trembling.

'Are you not well?' she asked quickly.

'I am well, thank you, Señora Brooks, but I have great worries.'

'Is it the store?'

'No, señora, it is my son in St Lucia. There is cholera in his village.'

'Then he must leave it at once.'

He shook his head. 'He is not allowed to leave. No one from his village may leave, for they might spread the infection.'

'It must indeed be a terrible anxiety for you,' she said kindly. 'I hope you will hear good news of your son soon. If he is young and healthy, all may be well with him.'

'The sickness strikes the young and old, healthy and weak.'

'Then we must pray for him,' she said gently. 'It is in God's hands.'

He murmured, 'Thank you for your sympathy, Señora Brooks,' and turned away.

Later that day Melia came to say, 'Geira don't give you the right soap, ma'am. I think he makes mistakes because he worried so much about his son. He leave the island this night, you know, and take boat to St Lucia.'

'But that is dangerous,' Triona exclaimed. 'He may catch the infection.'

'He go because he the boy's father,' Melia said, shaking her turbaned head. 'Parents is like that, you know.'

The next day Triona told the house-boy to bring round the carriage. The desire to see Duncan was too strong to be resisted any longer.

He was not in the house. His boy told her he had gone up to the sugar-mill. Triona gathered up the skirts of her thin gown and set off along the path to where the stone sugar-mill lay. She had come this way the night of the storm, riding behind Duncan and clinging to his hard body as the wind lashed them. Other memories came, unbidden and frighteningly vivid. She had gone half-way when she saw him coming towards her.

'Triona, I did not know you had come.' He looked down at her, his dark brows drawn in a frown. 'Is anything the matter?'

'Yes, I—I have been anxious . . . I had to see you.' Her heart was racing, making her so breathless that her words came jerkily. 'Norah has told me about that man.

Felix Craig, who has returned to Trinidad . . . and why he has come. Duncan, surely it is not possible you could be tried now when you were not accused then?'

A light flared in his eyes as he stared at her. 'So you do not think I am a murderer?'

'Oh no, no! Somewhere there is the real murderer. He must be found.'

His smile was wry. 'That is easier said than done. Felix has always hated me. He was fanatically devoted to his sister, and was convinced I killed her.' A muscle in his bronzed cheek twitched, and a sudden look of pain crossed his set face. 'He did his best at the inquest to get me accused. I didn't know, until Norah told me, that he had returned to Trinidad.'

She looked down, twisting the rings on her fingers nervously as she said, 'But if this man, Craig, has bribed the servants who originally testified to your being out fishing with them that night—if he should get them to lie and say you forced them to say what they did, will they be believed?'

He shrugged his shoulders. 'That lies in the lap of the gods. A jury is a strange and unpredictable thing. Wife-murder is not unknown in these islands; it is the betrayed husband's usual way of punishing his faithless wife. It was known Angela had given me cause for jealousy.'

'Were you—Were you fond of her?'

'If I had been in love with her, I might have killed her,' he said grimly. 'She killed my love after two months of our marriage. Perhaps people did not know that.'

'But she had lovers. If she had thrown them over and they had been jealous . . . There was a Spanish boy, Manuel something . . .'

His face hardened. 'Manuel Casulla. Young and passionately in love. Yes, he would have been suspected—if he had not left the island two days before the crime.'

'Duncan,' she caught his arm. Blood seemed to drain from her heart as she looked up into the lean face of the man whose love she had rejected, the man for whom she had tried so hard to convince herself she felt nothing but indifference. 'I—I'm afraid for you, terribly afraid!'

'Afraid for me?' his voice was harsh with pain. 'Why should you care what happens to me?'

Cold fear had turned to a burning fire in her. 'Duncan—I do care . . .'

'Dear me, do I interrupt something?' Neither of them had heard Flora approach. She stood watching them, a faint, mocking smile on her lips as her dark eyes went from Duncan's face to Triona's hand on his arm. Her voice, cool but with an edge to it, went on, 'I'm afraid I did not realise who . . . I had not supposed Mrs Brooks would be visiting you, Mr Ross. Effie and I called to ask about a gardener, but if we had known you had a visitor . . .'

With a supreme effort, Triona recovered her composure. 'But how strange, Mrs Ellison, that you did not notice my carriage before the house.'

'Oh, if I did, I would never have dreamed you would be calling *alone* on Mr Ross. In the circumstances it *is* a trifle strange, is it not?' She smiled at Duncan, her eyes soft and appealing. 'Mark is weary of female company, so I must beg you to dine with us tonight. I know you will come, just to please *me*.'

'I must go. Goodbye, Duncan.' Triona walked away, her head high and her eyes blazing. Not for worlds would she let Flora see the raging jealousy that was tearing her. She walked blindly, seeing nothing but Flora's seductive smile and hearing her soft, feline voice.

I hate her! The words blazed in her mind. *I hate her!*

Duncan! When had he become important to her? Why had she been so deeply dissatisfied when he accepted her dictum that only friendship must exist between them? She knew now, with terrible clarity, that she had wanted him to refuse to believe her, to declare his love and force her to declare hers!

She tried to stem the torrent of emotion that threatened to engulf her, but to no avail. It had broken its banks and swept away all the pretences she had erected to hide the truth. Duncan was dear to her!

During the days that followed, all her thoughts were with Duncan. Would his brother-in-law succeed in calling for a trial? Would Duncan tell her if he was called to Trinidad, or would she discover it through Norah?

Restless and uneasy, aware of the increasing strength of her feelings for the man she had once disliked, she could settle to nothing. Was it true, or had Flora invented it, that he had expressed the wish that she should return to England? The lovely widow made it obvious she found Duncan attractive, but there was no way of knowing how deep her feeling was, and it was possible it was deep enough for her to try to remove someone she considered a rival.

A letter came from her aunt. She wrote: 'Dearest Triona, I think so often of your sad plight in being alone in a strange land and being as yet unable to find a buyer for the estate. Once Forest Estate is sold, you must return to England; there is nothing but a sad memory for you in Ste-Martine. You have been very brave, my dear child, but I have sometimes been able to read between the lines of your letters, and I suspect the life of a planter did not suit Colin and that difficulties may have arisen. I long for you to return and start a new life unshadowed by unhappy recollections.'

Triona put the letter down and let her eyes wander to the window and the blaze of purple bougainvillaea and scarlet hibiscus. A life unshadowed by recollections? In

time Colin would fade to a sorrowful, pitying memory.
But the island held other memories for her; could she
ever forget them?

She drove into the town, more for filling the afternoon
than for any set purpose. On a sudden impulse she went
into the little church and found Mrs Fisher industriously
polishing brasses.

'Let me help you,' she said. 'Truly, I have nothing else
to do this afternoon. Could I polish some of the wood-
work, Mrs Fisher? Please let me.'

Mrs Fisher wiped her hand across her damp forehead
and looked at Triona thoughtfully before nodding and
saying, 'Indeed you can, my dear. It's warm work, but
the results are cheerful. I like to see things shining.
You'll find rags and polish in that basket, and you shall
come back to tea with me when we've done.'

The vicarage was shaded by a wide mango tree and
pleasantly cool. A small, pig-tailed girl staggered in with
the tea tray, and would have dropped it if Triona had not
gone to the rescue.

'I got her from the orphanage,' Mrs Fisher sighed. 'I
felt it was my duty, but she's a sad trial.' She examined
the tray. 'She's forgotten the slop-basin.' She raised her
voice to call, 'Ernestine!' She looked at Triona ruefully.
'The names they give them. I don't know how long I can
stand her.'

'I expect she will learn in time,' Triona said sooth-
ingly.

'I certainly hope so,' her hostess said grimly. 'When I
was entertaining Mrs Winkworth to tea, I had to tell
Ernestine to bring the slop-basin, and what must the
wretched child do but romp in with the *slop-pail!* Mrs
Winkworth did not seem amused.'

Mr Fisher came in as they were finishing, and fresh tea
was brought. He seated himself beside Triona and asked

how she was progressing in trying to sell the estate. When she reported failure, he shook his head gloomily, 'I greatly fear it will not be easy to sell it, Mrs Brooks. The island is too small to attract business men, and it may be a very long time before . . .'

'Don't be so discouraging, Ernest,' his wife said. 'Someone will snap it up one of these days.'

'I very much doubt it.'

'Yes, dear, you usually do, but I do not. The plantation could be sold to an adjoining estate and the house sold to some of the people who may be coming here if this agricultural project you mentioned comes about.'

'True, there does seem to be a possibility that the government may consider starting an experimental station for the study of tropical agriculture,' he agreed. 'But it is all in the air at the moment.'

'Then it had better come down to earth,' his wife declared firmly. 'We need something like that in Ste-Martine. It will bring more people.'

Triona went home slightly comforted. Surely if there had been news of a possible trial of the Ross case, the Fishers would have heard something of it. She told herself that Felix Craig had failed and was probably on his way back to England, a thwarted man.

As she came in sight of the house, she felt her heart leap. Duncan was swinging himself down from his horse and tossing the reins to the house-boy. She let him help her from the carriage, the touch of his hand setting her pulse leaping.

'Do come in, Duncan. I have been taking tea with the Fishers.' She led the way into the house, pulling off her hat. 'They were telling me . . .'

He interrupted her. 'I am going to Trinidad on the next boat.'

She swung round to stare at him. 'Duncan—not because . . .'

'No, I have heard nothing yet. But I do not mean to let Craig pervert justice if I can help it. I am going to face him and his accusations.'

'But all will—will be well, won't it, Duncan? You are innocent, everyone knows it.'

He said slowly, 'No, there are many people who believe I killed Angela and escaped trial by a lucky fluke. There well may be a trial if Craig is determined enough. I have come to say goodbye, Triona.'

'*No!*' She ran to him, gripping his arm. 'If there *is* a trial, you will be acquitted, I know you will! The true culprit will be found.'

'After four years?' he asked bitterly. 'He has vanished, but I am here, the husband of a faithless wife who was about to leave him for another man. My servants may say they lied.'

'But they didn't.'

His jaw tightened. 'Craig's money might convince them they did.' He was looking down at her, looking deep into her shocked eyes as he said slowly, 'You must know you are the only woman in the world for me, Triona—but you must forget me.'

'Duncan, I cannot! I—I . . .' The words choked in her throat as she looked up into his face, seeing the lines of strain there and the frightening resolution in his eyes, as he said.

'Now you are free, I had hoped . . . But I am not free and I never shall be. I will ask no woman to share the shadow that has darkened my life. Goodbye, Triona.'

He caught her to him, burying his face in her bright hair. She felt his body shudder, then he had released her and she was alone.

She subsided into a chair. So it had come, the thing she

had secretly dreaded. Duncan had left her. Even if there was no conviction, suspicion would always cling and the shadow be there, the shadow he would never let her share.

During the days that followed, her thoughts were all of Duncan. Her restlessness became a torment and her sleep fitful and dream-haunted. Suddenly she could bear it no longer. There would be no peace for her, no rest or easing of her fears until she was with him to share whatever might befall. The love that had grown so secretly and surely was something she had never felt for Colin. Her love for Duncan was a fire burning in her veins and driving out all thought but to be with him.

She drove into Regina. At the shipping office they told her that a boat was due to sail to Port of Spain in two days, and she engaged a cabin. Then she went to the Grantley house and found Norah at home and told her what she had done.

Norah nodded, and said quietly, 'You are right to go to him; he needs you now. You are a brave girl and my prayers will go with you. Go to Prince's Hotel; it is clean and they will look after you. Let me know your news when you have any, my dear.'

When she reached home, the turmoil of her thoughts drove Triona from the house and, catching up a parasol, she took the path that led to the cocoa plantation. The sky was bleached by noonday heat. New growth was springing up with tropical fecundity as the earth, refreshed by recent rains, was bursting into vigorous new life. Already creepers and vines were covering the fallen trees that had been felled by the hurricane, and suckers were shooting up from the broken banana palms.

She stopped to speak to Ram, who was hoeing the vegetable patch, and then thought she would walk a little way into the forest. Strolling in the pleasant shade, she heard a twig snap behind her and saw a man following her. She recognised Lew Corby.

He smiled, his teeth flashing white in his dark face where the scar on one cheek showed a dull red. Triona felt her heart begin to beat uncomfortably fast, but she allowed no sign of her uneasiness to show as she faced him to ask coolly, 'Do you wish to speak to me?'

He bowed with the mock deferential air she disliked and mistrusted. 'I ask your pardon for intruding, Mistress Brooks. I wish to offer my sincere sympathy on the tragedy of your husband's death. I have been out of the island and only now hear of this unhappy event.'

She thanked him coldly and turned away. She would have liked to walk back to the house, but he barred her way. His voice arrested her.

'Before your husband died so sadly, he offered me the position of overseer. I shall be happy to take that position, Mistress Brooks. A woman cannot manage an estate such as this without help. There is much work to be done.'

'Thank you.' She looked away, disliking the expression on his narrow face. 'But I intend to sell Forest Estate.'

He smiled unpleasantly as he murmured, 'I fear it will not be easy to sell it. It is not a good estate; it has been neglected and the hurricane has done damage. You will find a buyer soon, you think? *I* do not think so.'

'I do not agree.'

'You need someone who will see to remaking the plantation so it will attract a buyer.'

She raised her chin, looking him straight in his watchful eyes as she said, 'I do not need your services, Mr Corby.'

'You are a woman living alone . . .'

'I am not alone. I have my servants, and they are within call.'

'Ah yes, the ever-faithful Ram.' His face changed. 'How . . . unfortunate if anything should happen to him.'

She drew a quick breath as anger rose in her. 'If anything should happen to Ram, I shall know who is responsible. Goodbye, Mr Corby.'

He did not move. His eyes raked her from her vivid hair to her feet with an insolence that burned her. He looked up at the tree above him, a tree blazing with brilliant blossoms that glowed like small tongues of flame.

'The Flame of the Forest,' he murmured. 'So beautiful . . . but not so beautiful as you!'

Anger drove out her fear. Her eyes blazed as she walked towards him.

'You are insolent! Let me pass!'

For a moment he did not move, then he stepped back.

'I shall not say goodbye, Mistress Brooks. We shall meet again, I think.'

She walked on, giving no hint that she heard. She did not hurry but walked steadily, anger hot in her veins and her eyes dark and stormy. How dare he speak to her like that! He was loathsome—and dangerous.

Suddenly she saw Ram approaching, his cutlass swinging in his hand. He said, 'The sun grows warm, mistress. Is better you go back to the house, I think.'

'Ram,' she asked abruptly. 'I have just met that man, Lew Corby. Did you know he had followed me?'

'I have seen him. I did not know he returns to the island.'

'Ram, he said something—He does not like you, and I want you to be careful.'

The Indian's brown face did not change. 'I am careful. He is bad.'

'I shall keep the doors locked. I think I shall tell the police to warn him off the estate.'

'Yes, mistress. Corby don't like police. They think maybe he stab a man once-time.'

'They *think*? Don't they know?' she asked sharply.

'No, mistress. Only two-three people know, perhaps.'

She looked at him quickly, but his eyes slid away from hers. 'Ram, do *you* know . . .'

But he had bowed and slipped away among the palms.

CHAPTER
THIRTEEN

DAWN WAS painting the sky rose-pink and gold when the house-boy drove Triona down to the harbour, where she went aboard a neat little sailing ship, the *Carib Queen*. She stood on the deck as it pulled away from the jetty that had been hastily rebuilt after the hurricane, watching the little town slowly dwindle to a bright patch among the green of the forest where occasionally a scarlet patch flamed, the lovely Flame of the Forest. Unbidden, Duncan's words came back to her: 'Your hair—it is the colour of the immortelle . . . I have never before seen a woman with hair like yours . . .'

Soon the island had shrunk to a small green jewel set in sapphire seas, the island which had brought her pain, deep unhappiness and fear, and a love that had filled her heart and turned her from an inexperienced girl to a woman whose passionate love could match that of the man she was joining, the man whose future was in jeopardy.

The hours dragged for her. The ship's pace was a snail's pace to her impatient mind as she sat apart from the other passengers in a sheltered spot on deck, too absorbed in thought to be aware of the heat and dazzling glare from the sea around her.

She recalled her first meeting with Duncan in the Cunard office, and her reaction to his abrupt manner. Had she disliked him because some instinct warned her that danger might lie in liking him too much? She had told Colin she did not wish to be friendly with this blunt, ungracious man, and had thought it true. Why had she not seen that her dislike was a defence against the strong feelings he aroused in her?

The night of the hurricane had revealed much to her, but she had turned away from it, not daring to acknowledge the love that lay hidden deep in her heart. Now that love would be denied no longer; it filled her with aching desire and a terrible fear for the safety of the man who had come to mean everything to her.

There were still people who believed Duncan was guilty and saw him as a jealous husband who had discovered a faithless wife about to run away with her lover. The evidence given by his own servants was flimsy, but it had saved him. But the absence of any other suspect left an ugly cloud of suspicion that had forced him to leave Trinidad. And now a vengeful man, who had nursed his hatred and bided his time, openly declared Duncan guilty of wife-murder and had brought influence and money to bear out his accusation.

How would Duncan receive her? Would he think her unwise to follow him and so court gossip and perhaps condemnation by her action?

'I do not care what people may think,' she told herself fiercely. 'I love him, and my place is with him. *He is not guilty!* The truth must come out, it *must*!'

At last the evening came when they were sailing between the small islands known as the Bocas—'The Dragon's Mouth'—which guarded the Port of Spain harbour.

A sailor carried her valise ashore and summoned a small horse-drawn carriage to take her to Prince's Hotel, which lay on the perimeter of a wide savanna ringed with tall palms. It was a long wooden two-storey building with balconies and great baskets of hanging ferns.

A woman in a bright cotton dress greeted her and showed her to a pleasant room with a view of the low range of green hills behind the town.

She awoke early next day and lay listening to the unaccustomed sounds of voices and traffic. After breakfast, she dressed, and was pinning on her hat when the maid came to say that a gentleman was waiting to see her.

She caught her breath. It must be Duncan! But how had he known she was here? And where she was staying? She hurried down the stairs to the lounge and saw him standing watching her.

'Triona!' He strode to her and caught her hands. 'You are really here? I couldn't believe it when I got Norah's note telling me where you would be staying.'

'Norah wrote to you? But when did you get it?' she asked breathlessly, feeling her heart leap at his touch.

'She gave it to a man coming on your boat and told him to deliver it to me personally last night. God bless her for it! Triona, why have you come?'

She looked up at him, seeing the lines of strain in his strong, tanned face, and felt her heart ache for him. 'I think you know why,' she said softly, and saw the light that blazed in his grey eyes and felt the fierce grip of his fingers on hers.

For a long minute he was silent, looking intently at her. At last he said, 'Then it is true, what I've longed and prayed for. You have come to me at last, my dear one, my most beloved Triona!'

'Yes.' She met his gaze steadily. 'I have come to you, Duncan.'

'I still cannot believe it.'

She smiled. 'You once told me you meant to have me.'

'Yes, and I . . .' Abruptly his face changed, darkening as he dropped her hands and stepped back. 'That was before all . . . this business.'

'Duncan, my dearest,' she said swiftly. 'It does not make any difference to us. If you love me . . .'

'I love you enough not to let you tie yourself to a man under suspicion of being a murderer.' He spoke harshly, his eyes stern and bleak and all joy gone from his face.

'But you are not guilty!' She caught his arm. 'You have not committed any crime! Somewhere there is the true murderer, and he *must* be found!'

He said nothing for a minute. When he spoke, there was something in his voice that tightened her nerves. 'You had better know that the boys who were my servants are now prepared to swear I bribed them to say I was out fishing with them that night the crime was committed.'

She gasped. 'But how can they say such a thing now? What has made them . . .' Her words died as she remembered what Norah had said. 'Felix Craig!'

'Yes. He has always hated me for marrying his sister. He is convinced I killed her and means to see that I pay for it. He is obsessed with the desire for revenge—and unfortunately he has influence, both in London and here, and he is wealthy.'

'But justice . . .' She faltered as she saw his grim smile.

'Justice takes strange forms in these islands, Triona.'

'He has bribed the servants.'

He nodded. 'I'm pretty certain of it, but it may be impossible to prove. Neither of the boys was a reliable servant, and I had reason more than once to be harsh with them.' He drew a watch from his pocket and looked at it. 'I must go.'

'I shall come with you.'

'No, my dearest, you must remain here. When there is news, I shall send it to you.' He looked at her as she strove to hide the fear that had driven colour from her face and hot tears to her eyes. Suddenly he caught her to him, crushing her against his body.

'Oh God, how I have longed for you, my beautiful, enchanting, Lady of Flame!' He bent his head and she felt his kiss send fire through her. Then he had gone, leaving her lost in fears and hopes.

She sat on the balcony outside her room, unable to relax or think of anything but the trial. How far had it gone, she wondered anxiously? Perhaps if she bought a paper . . . But Duncan would come to tell her. To-morrow he might bring the joyful news that Felix Craig's bribery had been discovered and that the case was over. She must pin her hopes on that.

The maid came to tell her that lunch was ready, and she went down to the dining-room and forced herself to eat. If Craig's design could, by a miscarraige of justice, succeed, would Duncan be imprisoned, or . . . She pushed her unfinished dessert away and rose from the table. He had spoken of his life being shadowed; had he deliberately refrained from revealing what would be his fate if he were declared guilty? She shivered, and saw the manageress looking at her.

As she left the room, the woman stepped forward to ask softly, 'Would you like some coffee, Mrs Brooks? I could send it to your room.'

'No—Well, perhaps I will have it, thank you.'

When the coffee came, there was a small glass of brandy beside it. So the woman had guessed why she was here. Soon everyone would know, and there would be gossip and sly amusement among the island wives who had so little to occupy their minds. None of it mattered;

nothing mattered now but for Duncan's name to be cleared and Felix Craig's plans for revenge to be crushed.

'Let him be cleared of all suspicion for ever,' she prayed. 'Let the truth be known.'

She did not see Duncan the next day, neither was there any message. She hired a carriage and drove up the hills behind the town, among cocoa plantations and, further inland, wide fields of sugar-cane. The island was beautiful. In the north were thickly wooded mountains which sloped gently down to the plain that stretched to the south where the famous Pitch Lake lay. The little villages of palm-thatched huts and patches of corn and mango trees were alive with children who stopped their play to stare solemnly at the carriage and the English lady who smiled at them. But the heat became oppressive, and she was glad to return to the hotel and the coolness of her bedroom. And still there was no news from Duncan.

Night came with tropical suddenness and the hills were hidden in velvety darkness. Insects blundered around the lamps and the cicadas began their rusty chorus.

She was sitting by her window when the house-boy brought her the letter. For a moment she was afraid to open it. But surely it must bring good news!

She tore the envelope open with trembling fingers, and read: 'The case has gone against me; Craig has seen to that. I am to be tried for the murder of my wife four years ago. Go home, Triona. Return to Ste-Martine at once. It is my greatest wish, and if you love me you will obey. Go back to Forest and wait; I shall send news. Triona, make things easier for me, I beg you, and leave Trinidad. All is not lost yet. Further evidence may come. Craig has not yet succeeded in having me convicted, only in having me tried. God bless you for coming—but go back to Ste-Martine. Duncan.'

She sat very still, stunned by the news. She knew now that, in spite of all her fears, she had thought Craig would fail in his efforts to have Duncan tried. The shock was so great that she was empty of feeling. A sense of unreality deadened the pain that would come later. She rose and began mechanically to pack her clothes. Duncan had commanded her to return to Ste-Martine, and she would obey. She could not help or comfort him now.

From the hotel porter she learned that the *Carib Queen* was due to leave for Ste-Martine the next day, and he assured her that she would have no difficulty in getting a passage in it.

'That ship take stores to Ste-Martine,' he explained. 'Few peoples go on it mostly. I arrange it that you is taken to the harbour tomorrow, madam.'

She remembered little of the return journey. Fear tore at her, making the trip a nightmare of pain. Duncan, if he were convicted, would never marry her. She had lost him. Even if he were to be acquitted, she knew he would refuse to let her share the ugly suspicion that would cling to him until the true culprit was found. But after so many years, how was that possible? Someone had killed the faithless Angela on a dark night and slipped away to hide and allow an innocent man to be accused of the crime.

When the ship docked at Regina, she drove straight to the Grantley house.

'My dear child!' Norah exclaimed, throwing her book aside and rising from her chair. 'I did not expect you back so soon . . .' She broke off and went swiftly to Triona. 'Something has happened. Sit down and tell me.'

Norah listened, her eyes widening in dismay as Triona, speaking with stiff lips, her hands gripped together to prevent their trembling, told her of the trial and Felix Craig's triumph. When all was told, Norah sat silent for some minutes. Then she straightened her plump shoulders and said,

'It is not the end of things, never think that, my dear. If Duncan has a good man to defend him he may scare the servant boys into confessing the truth—and if it was found that they had money, it could have come only from being bribed. We'll not despair. I've prayed for Duncan, and I'm a great believer in prayer. Now, you'll stay here with me . . .'

'No, thank you so much, dear Norah. I must return home. There may have been an offer for the estate . . .' She put her hand to her head. 'It is difficult to concentrate—but Duncan wished me to return.'

'I don't like to think of your being alone.' She slipped her arm around Triona's shoulders, saying warmly, 'Remember I am here to help in any way I can. It is cruel that you should be parted. You love him, don't you, Triona?'

'Yes,' Triona whispered. 'I think I have, for a long time. I would do *anything* to help him—but all I can do is to wait.'

The short twilight had faded into night by the time she reached home. Melia's broad grin of welcome disappeared and she said, 'Is you unwell, ma'am? You looks so pale and sad.'

'I am tired after my journey, Melia. Can you get me some supper?'

There was little sleep for her that night. Frightening images rose before her eyes to torture her, and when dawn at last came she rose and dressed and left the house to walk in the freshness of the morning.

Beauty lay all around her. The awakening sky was a pageant of palest green, pink and apricot. Growing sunlight flashed on leaf and flower and speared through the trees as she wandered along the path. A vivid hummingbird shimmered before a hibiscus bush and, high above her, tiny green parrots flitted in the treetops.

At last she remembered Melia's concern for her. The cook would be anxious when she found her mistress's bed empty. She turned and, as she did so, her foot struck something lying on the side of the path. It was Ram's cutlass.

For a moment, it meant nothing. Then she caught her breath as she saw the trampled vines and something white behind a big silk cotton tree. She went forward swiftly, parting the bushes, and saw the body in white shirt and trousers and, for a second, her heart seemed to stop.

'Ram!' She knelt beside him and saw the blood matting the hair on the back of his head. She tried to feel his pulse but her hand shook, and, leaping to her feet and gathering her skirts round her, she ran to the house, fear and horror filling her heart.

'Melia! Come—oh, come quickly! Ram . . . I think he is dead! In the forest! Someone has attacked him! Come quickly . . . Tell Sam to come too!'

She led the way. Melia bent over the inert body of the little gardener for a few minutes, then she straightened up.

'He ain't dead, ma'am, but he hurt bad. Someone hit him a strong strong blow on he head and he lose blood.'

'Take him to his hut. I shall send for the doctor. Sam, can you carry him?'

'Sam and me carry him, ma'am,' the cook said. 'You go to the house. We bring him, and Sam go ride for the doctor.'

Triona took a clean sheet and spread it on Ram's corn-husk mattress in his hut. The two servants carried the gardener in carefully and laid him down, and Sam went off for the doctor. Triona watched Melia's deft fingers pull away the shirt from a cruel wound and wash away the blood.

'He ain't bleeding now,' she said, looking up. 'It a good sign, you know, when he don't bleed no more. It not long since he been smash down; the blood ain't dry yet.'

'But who could have done such a thing?' Triona cried. Suddenly she knew the answer. Lew Corby! '. . . unfortunate if anything should happen to him.' She could hear his hateful silky voice and see the smile on his dark face as he said it. Corby, seeking vengeance, waiting for Ram in the forest and striking him down! Had Ram suspected that Corby was in the vicinity and gone looking for him?

'It was a nasty blow,' the doctor told Triona after he had finished treating the wound. 'But these Hindus are strong, Mrs Brooks, and he will recover. Have you any idea who attacked him?'

'Yes, I have,' she said firmly. 'Please report the attack to the police when you return to the town, doctor.'

He promised to do so, and left her. Melia meanwhile had made coffee and placed it, with pawpaw, bread and honey, on the table.

'You has had a nasty nasty shock, ma'am,' she told Triona. 'Please you eat something now. I make the coffee strong strong.'

'Melia, do you know how to nurse poor Ram?'

Melia's broad black face expressed affronted pride. 'I is a good nurse, ma'am. I nurse many sick peoples on this island and they gets well, the most of them. Ram is waking and asks to speak with you, please.'

Triona hurried to the hut and found Ram, his face a curious mauve-brown colour and his eyes restless with pain. He beckoned to her, and she bent to hear his whisper.

'Don't go . . . in forest, mistress. Stay . . . in house. Safe . . . in house.'

'Ram, was it Lew Corby?'

'I don't . . . see. I . . . hit from behind.'

'But why were you in the forest this morning?'

His eyes shut, and she feared he had fainted again. But he managed to murmur, 'I see him . . . last night in forest. He a . . . bad man.'

That night she and the two maids took turns sitting with the injured man. He became feverish and his voice rose, high and cracked, jabbering in Hindi and sometimes chanting a wailing song.

At midnight Melia insisted that Triona went to bed, and she was too drugged with weariness to refuse. She fell almost instantly into a heavy sleep that lasted until the cook brought the news that Ram was sleeping and had drunk some of the 'good good medicine' she had prepared.

Triona sat up. 'But the doctor said he was to have nothing until the fever left him!'

Melia sniffed contemptuously. 'White doctors don't know what is good for black peoples. I make bush tea that heals people, ma'am. Many times I make it for sick peoples and it do good, you know.'

Triona hoped sincerely it was true, and she had to admit that Ram was looking better and seemed free of pain when she went to see him. Either the cook's bush tea, or a firm belief in it, had helped him.

Later that morning a young police officer came, and she told him of the attack on Ram and the suspicion she had that the attacker had been Corby.

'Of course, if your man did not actually see who hit him,' the officer said cautiously, 'it won't be easy to accuse Corby. But of course I shall make enquiries about him and where he was last night, and so on.'

'Ram has asked me not to go far from the house,' Triona told him. 'He seems to think Corby is hanging around still and might be a danger to me.'

'Oh, I hardly think that, Mrs Brooks. But I shall certainly tell the man, when I find him, that he is not to put a foot on your estate. If he does, he will be arrested. That will keep him away.'

When he had gone—in the direction of the Ashtons' bungalow—Triona went to the window and stood looking out at the sun-drenched garden. Her mind was at rest about Ram, but her fears for Duncan had returned to torment her. Her longing for him grew so piercing, so overwhelming, that she could hardly bear it. What was the penalty for murder in these islands? Death? She shivered, clasping her cold hands to her breast. No, not death, probably, for a crime of passion presumed to have been committed by a man driven beyond reasoning by an adulterous wife. Prison, certainly, and a life for ever poisoned by the stigma of murder. Prison for a man such as Duncan Ross! A grim cage for a hawk which would bruise its wings against the bars.

'I must not despair,' she told herself fiercely. 'Justice may yet be done. Craig's treachery may be found out. He has lied and bribed to distort the path of justice; surely there are honest men who will question his motives? Men who remember Duncan and *know* he is not a murderer.'

If only she could help him, but all she could do was to wait and pray. There was no further news from Trinidad. Ste-Martine was too small to do much trading with other islands. Triona did not go into the town lest she meet people who would want to discuss the trial with her.

Ram continued to improve under Melia's ministrations. He had no answer to the question of who attacked him, but Triona knew he suspected Corby. The wound had healed well and he was able to tend the vegetables that Sam would be taking into the market.

She was writing to her aunt when she saw the Ashton carriage drive up, and rose as the servant showed Effie into the room, glad to have her thoughts diverted.

'How nice to see you, Mrs Ashton. Do have some coffee, or would you prefer a lime drink?'

'Thank you so much, Mrs Brooks, but I mustn't stop. Mark's cousin, Harry Drew, who has been cruising in these waters, brought his yacht into Regina harbour last night and is to spend some days with us.'

'How pleasant for you,' Triona said with a smile.

'Oh yes, it is. But,' she came close to Triona and her voice dropped to a whisper. 'He has come from Trinidad and has brought such dreadful news! Poor Mr Ross has been tried for the murder of his wife four years ago and has been found guilty! It seems his alibi—is that what it is called?—has been disproved, and the evidence against him is *very* strong, because his wife was going to elope with her lover. Mrs Brooks, are you feeling all right?'

Triona had sunk into a chair as the room began to spin around her. She felt herself slipping into a black void . . .

She opened her eyes to find herself lying on the sofa with Melia bathing her face with cold water while Effie hovered near.

'Oh dear! I should not have told her so abruptly! He was a friend, and it has been a dreadful shock. Will she be all right? Is she . . .'

'She done faint, ma'am,' Melia said. 'She come all right now.'

'I'm so sorry.' Triona tried to sit up, but was firmly prevented by Melia. 'It was stupid of me. It is the heat, I expect.'

'It is all my fault,' Effie said remorsefully, 'to have given you such a shock.'

'Is it true?' Triona felt her throat tighten. 'It is all so terribly wrong! Duncan is innocent, surely everyone must know that? He did not—he *could* not—have killed his wife!'

'Oh no, of course he could not,' Effie agreed uneasily. 'But the evidence against him . . . Pray, do not worry, dear Mrs Brooks, I expect they will find that his servants were lying.'

Melia, who had disappeared, now returned with a small glass in her hand. 'Is a small bit of brandy.' She eyed Effie coldly. 'I does think it better Mistress Brooks rests now and don't bother with words till she feeling better, ma'am.'

'Oh yes, of course. I'm so *dreadfully* sorry! It was so stupid and unkind of me, but I never meant to . . . If there is anything I can do . . .'

'Ain't nothing *I* can't do, ma'am.' Melia's words had a finality that sent Effie out of the house. Triona obediently drank the brandy and allowed the cook to put a cold compress on her forehead and lower the shutters to keep out the brilliant light.

It had come, the news she had been dreading! Felix Craig had succeeded, by what means she could only guess at, in pinning the crime on Duncan, the man he hated. But Duncan was innocent, and innocent men were not condemned. Someone would challenge the verdict, someone who knew Duncan and knew that justice had been perverted.

Her head ached cruelly and she lay with closed eyes, trying to will herself to calmness. As soon as she felt less shaky, she would go to Norah and find comfort in her warm and optimistic nature.

Melia protested when Sam was told to get the carriage, but Triona paid no heed to the cook's dire warning that she might faint again.

Norah was outside the house when Triona drove up. She called, 'I was just about to drive out to you. Come inside.'

Triona followed her into the pleasantly cool sitting-room, which was delicately scented by a vase of gardenias.

'You have heard?' she asked in a tight voice.

Norah nodded. 'I met Effie Ashton and her husband's cousin, Captain Drew, in the town. Did she call on you?'

'Yes.'

'The silly little gossip. She has never learned when to hold her tongue.'

'I would have heard eventually,' Triona said wearily. 'Everyone will soon know.'

'There, my dear. We'll have coffee and talk about this.'

Triona sat down. 'It *cannot* be true,' she whispered. 'I will not believe it.'

'My dear, you must be brave and face it. Justice has been perverted, and we are powerless to fight the evil that has made it so.' Norah seated herself beside Triona and took her hand. 'It will mean prison, not—the other thing. It will be assumed that it was a crime of passion against an adulterous wife. And there must still be some doubts about Duncan's guilt.'

'There are no doubts.' Triona spoke dully. A numbness was stealing over her. This was some ghastly nightmare. It was not real, it *could* not be real. *'Duncan is innocent.'*

'Triona dear, *we* know that, but . . .' Norah raised her head. 'Did I hear someone come in?'

'I cannot meet anyone,' Triona exclaimed in panic. 'Send them away, whoever they are, Norah!'

Norah hurried to the door and Triona heard her say, 'I am not at home to anyone today.'

The maid's voice broke in, protesting shrilly, 'I done tell he that, ma'am, and you has a lady visitor, but he don't pay no 'tention.'

A man's voice said, 'I must see you, Señora Grantley, and Señora Brooks too. It is of the greatest importance that I see you before I leave the island.'

Triona had risen at the sound of his voice. As she took a step towards a door leading to the veranda, Juan Geira burst into the room, exclaiming,

'You must hear me! You are both his friends! You must hear me!'

She turned reluctantly and was shocked at what she saw. The Spaniard had aged cruelly. His face was grey and etched with lines of pain, and his deeply sunken eyes held such stark tragedy that Norah instinctively motioned him to a chair.

With an effort at composure, Triona asked, 'Your son? I hope he has recovered.'

'My son is dead.'

'Oh, how terribly sad for you. You have my sympathy.'

'What a tragedy,' Norah said. 'I am very sorry.'

He bowed his head as he said, 'I thank you, ladies. But I do not come to speak only of his death.' For some minutes he remained silent as if seeking strength for what he had to say. His eyes went to a packet he held, and at last he raised his head and spoke.

'I was with my son when he died. Before he was taken from me, he signed a confession. It was witnessed by three people, one a member of the police force. I have it with me.'

'A confession?' Triona exclaimed. 'I don't understand. What did your son confess to, Señor Geira?'

The old man's face twisted in sudden pain. 'To the murder of Señor Ross's wife in Trinidad four years ago!'

CHAPTER
FOURTEEN

TRIONA SAT frozen into immobility, her eyes wide and the colour slowly draining from her face as she stared at the old man sitting with bowed head before her. It was Norah who spoke first.

'*Your son?* But he did not know her!'

'He knew her,' Juan said heavily. 'He was her lover.'

'The Spanish boy!' Norah exclaimed. 'But he was Manuel Casulla!'

'He is—he was—my son.' The man seemed to make an effort to collect his thoughts. 'I was in some political trouble when I left Spain and I took another name, but my son did not. He was in Trinidad when Señor Ross brought his young wife there.'

Triona sprang to her feet, joy and hope sweeping over her. 'At last, the truth! Duncan is free after all he has suffered!' She turned fiercely on Juan, her eyes blazing. 'Why didn't your son confess before? Why did he let an innocent man be suspected of murder when he knew himself to be the murderer?'

'My son was not a true murderer.' Pain and anger made his voice rough. 'He was a man who loved passionately a woman who swore she loved him and who threw him over when she tired of him. In Spain, it would be understood that such a man may take revenge on a faithless woman.'

'But I still don't understand,' Norah said. 'Manuel

Casulla had left the island *before* the murder.'

'That is true.' Life seemed to go out of the old man, and he sagged in his chair. 'When he realised the woman was a deceiving harlot, he went to Venezuela. But his passion was too strong. He took a boat and returned to Trinidad at night—it is not so distant—and went to Señor Ross's house to plead once more with the woman who had become a fire in his blood, and there he learned she planned to go to a wealthy lover that night. She laughed at my son's love! She taunted him with his youth and inexperience as a lover! His love, thrown back at him, turned to hate and for a moment he was indeed mad. His mind turned dark and he lost all reason . . . and he killed her!'

Norah gasped, then said, 'But he wasn't found on the island.'

'He hid in the Caroni mangrove swamps south of Port of Spain, where he had hidden his boat. The swamps are used by those who wish to escape the law. When a black night comes, he returns to the mainland. Later he comes to St Lucia and makes himself a good business there.'

'Did you know what he had done?' Triona asked accusingly.

He shrugged. 'I had—some little suspicion, yes. But Señor Ross was not accused . . . and he was my son.'

'But when Mr Ross was called for trial, what then?'

'Then, ah yes, I am much worried. When my son becomes ill, I go to him and he confesses all; and I make him write it, and it was witnessed before he died.' He rose slowly, gripping his packet of papers. 'Now I shall wait for a ship to take me to Trinidad. The law cannot harm my son now, he is in the hands of God, and God will judge him.'

Triona suddenly cried, 'Wait!' She looked at Norah.

'The yacht that belongs to Mark Ashton's cousin, is it still here?'

'Yes, in the harbour.' Norah's face was alight with excitement. '*He* must take Juan to Trinidad! I'm sure when he knows how important it is, he will agree. Come, we'll go to the Ashtons immediately and you, Juan, go home and prepare to leave at once.'

The tall bearded young man whom Mark introduced as Captain Drew, listened intently to Triona's explanation and, when she had done, immediately agreed to sail for Trinidad and take Juan with him.

'We're ready to set sail,' he told her. 'I planned to leave the day after tomorrow. I'm only too pleased to be able to see that justice is done. Mr Ross has been most cruelly treated. Who is this fellow Craig who has hounded him so?'

'Don't waste time, old chap,' Mark Ashton urged him. 'Effie will see to your packing while I order the carriage. If I wasn't tied up with work, I'd go with you. Ross is a fine fellow and has had more than his share of suffering.'

Captain Drew did not waste time. Half an hour later, he and Mark Ashton set out for Regina to find Juan and take him aboard the yacht.

When they had gone, Effie seated herself, fanning her flushed face. 'Such excitement! To think it was that horrid Spanish boy all the time! Why, poor Mr Ross might have been hanged, or imprisoned for life!'

'Well, he won't be either,' Norah said, crushing Effie's flight into melodrama. 'And I think I'd like something strong to drink. I feel quite shaky after all this.'

Flora, who had been unusually silent during the proceedings, suddenly remarked, 'I feel perfectly shocked when I think of poor Mr Ross's ordeal! Of course I have always known he was *completely* innocent.'

'Indeed you haven't,' her sister-in-law said with some

asperity. 'I heard you telling that young police officer that Duncan Ross was just the type of rough, cold-natured man you could imagine becoming violent.'

'I did not—At least, I . . .' Flora hesitated, biting her lip, then turned and swept out of the room.

'Changes her mind pretty quickly, doesn't she?' Norah remarked.

'Yes, she does,' Effie said, looking ruffled. 'Between ourselves, I think it is time Flora went home. She is not an easy guest. And that poor young police officer is getting far too attached. If he thinks she has the least interest in him, he is sadly mistaken. Flora has always been a flirt; she cannot exist without male admiration. Why, she has been making eyes at Harry, who is married. His wife is staying with some friends in Port of Spain. Dear Mrs Brooks, you look so pale. Are you feeling quite well?'

Triona aroused herself from her whirling thoughts. 'It is only the shock,' she murmured. 'It has happened so swiftly that I can hardly believe it yet that Duncan will return to me a free man.'

Effie sent a startled glance to Norah, who nodded and smiled. Then she said, 'Oh, I didn't realise . . . But of course I should have guessed! Indeed you must be terribly relieved and happy, Mrs Brooks—but may I call you Triona, it is such an unusual name? I'll tell you a little secret: Flora has been very jealous of you! She tried her wiles on Duncan Ross, but he didn't respond as she expected and she blamed it on you. I once heard her say something quite unkind, and untrue, about you to him, and I took her to task about it afterwards. There hasn't been much love lost between us since then.'

'She told me something Duncan said to her,' Triona told her. 'It was that day we went across the island to the west coast.'

Effie sat up, her pretty little face flushed. 'She told me, too, that he had expressed the wish for you to return to England. I accused her of making it up, and she confessed she had, and laughed when I said it was perfectly horrid of her. Flora is unscrupulous when she wants something. I shall *not* be sorry when she leaves us.'

'I am spending the day with you,' Norah announced when she and Triona had returned to Forest House. 'I couldn't sit alone after all this excitement. Are you truly happy now, my dear?'

Triona drew a long quivering breath before replying. 'It is like coming out of a great choking black cloud of fear and misery into sunlight.'

'Ah, I'm so happy for you both. He'll be back to claim you just as soon as he can. Have you any plans? But how could you, with this hanging over you. I wonder will Duncan want to remain in the West Indies.'

'Wherever he goes, I shall go,' Triona said passionately. 'My only wish is to be with him for ever. Tomorrow I shall write to my aunt and tell her everything.'

'Will she be shocked?' Norah asked doubtfully. 'She doesn't yet know what your life was with Colin, and she may consider you are being a trifle hasty in marrying again so soon.'

'She will be surprised, I know. But she always knew poor Colin was weak and I think she has suspected that the life here changed him greatly. About Duncan, I cannot guess. But I know she loves me and has always wished for my happiness.'

Norah nodded and said, 'And your happiness lies with Duncan.'

The news of Manuel Casulla's confession spread rapidly, and little else was discussed throughout the island. Norah, who was entertaining the Fishers to tea

when Triona called on her a few days later, remarked
caustically on the number of people who were now
saying they never really suspected Duncan Ross of the
murder.

'A funny way they had of showing it,' she remarked to
the vicar. 'Treating him like a pariah.'

'I am afraid human nature is not always kind,' he
sighed.

'I wonder what will happen to Felix Craig,' his wife
said. 'He must be a strange, twisted creature.'

'The Craigs are a strange family,' Norah told her.
'Felix was . . . unnaturally attached to his sister. Angela
was a woman completely without moral sense; and I've
heard there was at least one member of the family who
had to be put away. There's a bad strain in them.'

'He certainly ought to be punished for the way he
hounded poor Mr Ross.'

'I know what would happen to him if *I* got my hands on
him,' Norah said fiercely. 'And don't tell me to forgive
sinners, vicar, for that man is beyond forgiveness.'

'My dear Mrs Grantley, no man is beyond forgiveness . . .' the vicar began, but catching Norah's fiery
glance, decided silence was the better part.

They were interrupted by the arrival of the young
police officer.

'By jove, wasn't it splendid news?' he declared heartily, accepting a cup of lukewarm tea. 'If that Spanish boy
hadn't confessed, things would have been pretty nasty
for Duncan Ross.'

'When will he be able to return?' Triona demanded,
her eyes shining.

'Well, the law moves slowly, I'm afraid. Of course we
all know what the verdict will be now, but there will be
things to be tidied up, I expect.'

'We are all deeply grateful to Captain Drew,' she said

warmly, and was surprised to see the young man's face fall.

He sighed as he said, 'I believe he plans to set sail for England quite soon, and Mrs Ellison will return with him and his wife.'

'And a good thing too,' was Norah's comment when the stricken lover had departed. 'She would have ruined him if she had stayed. A heartless siren, but she didn't fool Duncan. She is no friend to you, Triona, but people have learned the type of woman she is and she's had more than one snub, as well I know.'

Triona rose, gathering up gloves and parasol as she said happily, 'I shall go home and wait, but this time I am waiting for joy and not for sorrow.'

The days that had been so long and fearful were days of golden happiness and hope for her now, and she sang as she went about the house. She drove to Toco and found Duncan's servants were looking after the house and estate.

When she met the young police officer in the town, she asked him if he had any news of Lew Corby, and was told he had produced an alibi for the night Ram was attacked.

'It isn't a very firm alibi,' he told her. 'Corby has certain influence over some of the people here, and many are scared of him. We are keeping an eye on him—at least we were,' he amended. 'He seems to have left the island; he isn't to be found in any of his old haunts. I think you need have no fear he will trouble you again, Mrs Brooks.'

'I hope not,' she said. 'He is a dangerous man. Did you know he once stabbed a man?'

'It was not proved; no witnesses came forward.'

'Because they were too frightened of him,' she pointed out. 'I think there *were* witnesses. I trust you are right in thinking Corby has left Ste-Martine, but you do not have proof of it yet, do you?'

'No actual proof,' he admitted. 'But he knows we are watching him, and it must have made him uneasy. He probably slipped away on one of the small fishing boats that call in here. Don't worry, Mrs Brooks.'

News of the trial came and, as was expected, Duncan was acquitted of the murder of his wife. To Triona, whose impatience mounted as the days passed, it seemed strange that the case took so long to end.

Mark Ashton, when he called with a message from Effie one morning, explained that the authorities had thought it necessary to bring to Port of Spain the police-man who had witnessed the confession.

'Thank heaven the whole thing is over for Ross,' he said. 'He has had a rough time since his wife was killed. He had to leave Trinidad because of the rumours, and he did not find things much better here.'

Effie's message was a request for Triona to go with her to Government House where Mrs Winkworth was hold-ing a ladies' tea-party. Triona had received an invitation, and was on the point of refusing it.

'Effie will be jolly upset if you don't go, Mrs Brooks,' Mark said earnestly. 'I'm afraid she and Flora aren't hitting it off very well these days and, well . . .'

'And I am to be a buffer between them,' Triona said, laughing. 'I'm not sure I am adequate for such a position.'

'Oh, but you are. Effie could chat to you instead of quarrelling with my sister, who is not in the best of moods for some reason. Do say you'll go, Mrs Brooks? Effie has a new dress she's dying to show off, but I doubt if she'll attend the affair without you. I expect your friend Mrs Grantley will be there.'

'I haven't a new dress, I'm afraid,' Triona told him,

smiling. 'But I will go if it means Effie's new creation will languish unseen if I don't. It is the day after tomorrow, isn't it? I shall write my acceptance right away.'

'Thank you, you're a brick, Mrs Brooks,' he said gratefully. 'I'll wait while you write it and take it with me when I go to town.'

'In case I should change my mind, I suppose,' she teased him. 'But a promise is a promise and I shall not fail Effie.'

It would give her something to do, she thought, while she waited for Duncan's return.

When she went out to meet the Ashton carriage, Triona noticed Flora's chilly greeting and was secretly amused by it. Effie, looking charming in misty blue muslin and cream lace, hailed her gladly.

'Dear Triona, I am so glad you've decided to wear white and not that stuffy black, and how pretty you look in that hat with the violets.'

'I am not sure Mrs Winkworth will approve,' Triona said, as the groom assisted her into the carriage.

'I would hardly expect her to myself,' Flora remarked, smoothing the ruffles on her magenta satin skirt. 'It is most unusual for a newly widowed woman to wear . . .'

Effie interrupted her sharply by saying, 'London ideas do not apply to the tropics, Flora. I wish you would not be for ever criticising people. You really know very little about life in these islands.'

'But I am learning,' Flora said smoothly. 'Some very . . . odd things can happen when conventions are disregarded. Women appear to be less discreet; they do not seem to cherish their sex's most precious jewel, their reputation.'

'Well, if it comes to *that*, my dear Flora . . .' Effie began, but Triona broke in quickly to ask,

'Do you think there will be many guests? Some

women here have given up the English habit of tea, I believe.'

'Well, I haven't,' Effie said firmly. 'Neither have you nor any sensible woman. I am hoping there will be a Planters' cake.'

'I'm afraid not,' Triona said. 'Norah Grantley says Mrs Winkworth considers nine eggs to be a wicked extravagance in a cake.'

For a moment, as they bowled up the drive to the house, Triona had a sudden, unhappy vision of the day she and a reluctant and sullen Colin had attended a garden party there. Then it had gone, and she was returning smiles and greetings with the brightly dressed crowd of women under the trees on the lawn. Long tables covered in white damask cloths were set out and servants moved smoothly to and fro with plates and trays of cakes.

Norah rustled up to her, exclaiming, 'It's good to see you here, Triona. And how blooming you're looking in that pretty white muslin. Your hostess is by the jacaranda tree. She'll give you two fingers and a sour smile because you're not hung with black crepe and jet, but don't mind the poor woman, she has little to do but disapprove of us.'

Rather to her surprise, Triona found the Honourable James Winkworth at her side.

'May I get you a chair, Mrs Brooks?' he asked, and signalled a servant. 'We do not see you very often, I fear. I hear you are selling Forest Estate. Has a buyer turned up yet, may I ask?'

'I am afraid not.'

'It is unfortunate, perhaps, that Toco Estate is also for sale,' he said. 'It is, I fear, a more saleable property. Ross looked after it well and made much improvement to the crops.'

Triona caught her breath. 'I did not know Toco was to be sold.'

'Oh yes, it was put in the hands of agents when Ross went to Trinidad. Under the then circumstances, he probably thought he would not—er—be returning to it.'

'But now he is returning a free man . . .'

'I understand he has not withdrawn the sale,' he said. 'After what has happened, he may not wish to remain in the West Indies. Life has been difficult for him— Rumours, you know, and people talking.'

'And people unjustly condemning him!' she said hotly. 'People who believed the rumours, people without charity or pity!'

'Er, yes—quite so.' He rose hurriedly. 'I see Mrs Fisher approaching to talk to you. Very pleasant to see you, Mrs Brooks.' He walked away as Mrs Fisher came up.

Other friends came, and Triona listened and smiled while allowing her mind to speculate on Duncan's decision to sell Toco. He had not told her, probably because he did not wish her to know he feared the trial would go against him. Would he still wish to sell his estate when he returned? But he would tell her his plans when she saw him.

The wife of the Police Commissioner, a plump, gossipy, rather stupid little woman, was chatting at her side, happily unaware of any lack of attention. Suddenly her words broke into Triona's thoughts.

'. . . but of course it is *perfectly* understandable for him to wish to leave this part of the world, isn't it? I mean, after all he has suffered, what is more natural than he would go back to England once he is free to do so. He has written to my husband, you know, about selling the Toco Estate, and mentioned he would leave Trinidad for England when the case was finally cleared up. You

would think he might come back to see about the sale of
Toco himself, but probably he never wishes to see
Ste-Martine again.' She ended with a little laugh, and
began to move away.

'Wait!' Triona said sharply. 'You say Mr Ross wrote
to your husband that he did not intend to return to
Ste-Martine?'

'Oh yes. The letter came yesterday, and my husband
told me about it. So we shall not be seeing Mr Ross
again. It has all been quite like a novel, hasn't it?' She
tripped away.

Shock held Triona rigid. She had been unaware there
had been mail from Trinidad. Why had she not received
a letter from Duncan? He must know how deeply she
was longing to hear from him and when he would return.
The woman was wrong, she must be wrong! Nothing
would keep Duncan from returning to the island and
her, the woman he loved and of whose love he was now
certain.

Despite the heat, she was suddenly cold. The woman
was mistaken, she repeated to herself, she had not
understood, or listened properly to, what her husband
had said. She pulled herself back from the brink of fear.
There was some ridiculous mistake; Duncan's love was
too strong ever to be shaken. She would not allow
herself to doubt it, no matter what she was told!

Effie was full of chatter on the drive home and did not
notice Triona's silence. They were alone, Flora having
chosen to be driven back by a young doctor who had
recently come out from Scotland to join the hospital
staff.

'When do you expect Captain Drew back from
Trinidad?' Triona asked abruptly.

'Oh, I don't think we shall see him again,' Effie told
her. 'He and his wife will wait in Port of Spain for Flora

to join them. She has found a boat going to Trinidad in a few days, and they will set off for England. Mark brought a splendid mail last week—I have two English magazines I shall lend you. He collected your mail also, I believe.'

'And delivered it; it was kind of him.'

'I believe there was a boat in from Barbados and Trinidad. Did you get news from Duncan?'

'I—No,' Triona said, looking away.

'Oh well, I expect he did not have the time to write and you will hear from him on the next boat in. Here we are at your house. Goodbye, Triona, and thank you for coming with me. It was a very pleasant afternoon, wasn't it? I don't suppose I shall see Flora for hours; she will be at the club with her latest conquest.' Effie waved as the carriage turned away.

Triona went into the house slowly, aware that the afternoon, for her, had not been pleasant. She took off her hat and lifted her hair from her damp forehead.

'Why am I bothering about stupid gossip?' she thought uneasily. *'I know I can trust Duncan. He loves me, and nothing will ever change that.'*

But suppose something had? The frightening thought crept into her mind, unbidden, and chilling her. What if the trauma of the last weeks had altered him, as it could well have altered a man who had suffered as he had? Was it possible that now his single desire, blotting out all else, was to leave the island where his life had been made so bitter, if he wanted to forget the past—and her?

CHAPTER
FIFTEEN

WHY HAD she not heard from Duncan?

The question burned itself into Triona's brain and haunted her dreams at night. He had written to the Commissioner of Police, and even if there had been little time to write, surely he could have written a short letter to assure her of his complete clearance and his longing to be with her. She was his love, the woman he wanted more than anything else in the world. She was sure of it—and yet a creeping doubt, seeping into her mind like a poison, was robbing her of her former joy. She despised herself for doubting him. She could not forgive herself such treachery, yet still the doubts grew as days passed and there was no letter.

She suspected that Effie knew something; she was uneasy when they met and kept the conversation on gossip about the tea-party at Government House. Did all the island think Duncan Ross did not mean to return to Ste-Martine?

It was impossible to imagine that he could be crushed by his experiences. He was a strong and resolute man. He had known he was innocent, and now it had been proved beyond all doubt and the shadows had retreated, the shadows he would not allow her to share.

Much as she longed for comfort, Triona did not go to Norah. She dreaded her questions—and her sympathy. She set herself resolutely to fight her fears and to wait, with all the calmness she could summon, for news and for Duncan's return.

Ram had made a good recovery from his attack by an unknown, but suspected, assailant. He worked industriously, and helped her with instructions to the few field workers she had kept on. She no longer felt any interest in the estate. With luck, she would sell it, even if she had to accept a poor price for it.

Ram came with a hand of bananas one morning and, on a sudden impulse, she asked him if he thought Lew Corby had left the island.

He shook his head. 'Is hard to say, Mistress Brooks. No one sees him now. May be he hides hisself when police come to make questions. He don't like police, so I think perhaps he takes a small ship to St Lucia. It is good if he goes; he is bad and says many bad lies.'

'What kind of lies, Ram?' she asked him.

He ran a brown finger along the blade of his cutlass before replying, 'He is saying he buys Forest from you, Mistress Brooks, because no body will buy it and he will pay a small price for it. Is lies, lies, all the time with him.'

'He is certainly lying if that is what he says. I am very glad the police have frightened him off the island.'

'Yes, mistress.' He picked an ant off the hand of bananas he had placed on the kitchen table. 'I asks you if I can go away for one-two days, please.'

'Yes, Ram.' Knowing the usual reason for servants to wish some time off, she asked, 'Is it for a funeral?'

'No, mistress.' He looked coyly down at his sandalled feet. 'I get married to a wife.'

'Then of course you must go. Who is the bride?'

'She named Noona. She a big strong woman and will have many sons.'

She sat down to make a list of groceries needed from

the town, smiling at the gardener's unromantic description of his bride-to-be.

The house-boy had set off with her list, and she was drinking coffee and reading the newspapers that had come in the mail Mark Ashton had brought from the town for her, when she heard carriage wheels outside. A minute later she rose, surprised and not over-pleased to greet Flora Ellison, who rustled in smiling brightly.

'Good morning, Mrs Ellison,' Triona said, endeavouring to infuse welcome into her voice. 'Would you care for some coffee?'

'That would be delightful, Mrs Brooks. Is it not strange how much we enjoy a hot drink in this climate? I do not like fruit drinks, and lime juice quite upsets me, I fear. Effie has asked me to bring you the magazines she received recently. They are out of date, of course, which makes one realise how dreadfully isolated one is in a place like Ste-Martine.' She sat down. 'You know, I could *never* live in a place like this.'

'Well, luckily, there is no reason why you should, is there?' Triona said, and went to the door to order more coffee. As she turned, she caught Flora's glance, and her nerves suddenly tightened at something coldly amused in it. 'I believe you intend to join Captain Drew and his wife in Port of Spain and return to England with them?'

'So Effie has told you? Yes indeed, Harry was *so* insistent, I really could not refuse his offer of the trip home. It will be quite delightful, you know, I adore yachting. There will be the four of us, such a pleasant prospect.'

'Four? I thought . . . I thought only Captain Drew and his wife . . .'

'Oh, so did I at first. But now it appears Duncan Ross wishes to join our little party. One is not surprised that, after his terrible experiences out here and the cruel way he has been treated, he should wish to leave the West Indies and all it has done to try to ruin his life. Dear me, Mrs Brooks. Did that coffee scald your hand?'

'It is nothing.' Mechanically Triona wiped up the coffee she had spilled. 'Is it certain he means to return to England?'

'Oh yes, perfectly certain,' Flora assured her. She sipped her coffee, her eyes bright with malice. 'I have had a letter from him—it came in the mail from Trinidad a few days ago—and he told me he is selling his estate here and has no intention of returning. I feel *so* sorry for you, dear Mrs Brooks. I know he was a . . . very great friend.' She put down her cup and picked up her frilled parasol. 'But an experience such as Duncan has had changes a man's ideas, you know. He can never be the same afterwards; his only wish must be to forget the past as swiftly and completely as he can.' She rose gracefully, tucking a dark curl under the pretty little rose-trimmed bonnet. 'I really must leave you now, I have so much to do before I leave. Is there any message you would like me to convey to Duncan?'

Triona's eyes blazed suddenly as she said, 'No, thank you, Mrs Ellison. You see, I am not as convinced as you are that Mr Ross will not return to Ste-Martine.'

Flora's pretty teeth showed in a feline little smile as she murmured, 'Dear Mrs Brooks, I do understand how you feel. Such a disappointment for you . . . But these things do happen, don't they? Fate can be *so* unkind. Thank you so much for the coffee. As I may not be seeing you again, can I say goodbye to you?'

'Goodbye, Mrs Ellison,' Triona said briefly, ignoring the hand her guest extended. Flora hesitated, then with a little laugh she turned and left the room.

Triona waited until the sound of carriage wheels had

faded, then she dropped into a chair. *Was* it true? Had Flora truly received a letter from Duncan? Would she have gone so far as to tell a deliberate lie, a lie that could so easily be discovered? The purpose of her visit was obvious: she had triumphed, and wished Triona to know it. If she had not received a letter, she must be counting on her powers to persuade Duncan to accompany the Drews to England. But the Commissioner of Police had also had a letter from Duncan . . .

'I will not believe it!' she told herself fiercely. *'I will not believe it!'*

She did not go into the town in the days that followed. In spite of her decision not to call upon Norah, she missed her warm friendship and was somewhat surprised that she had not received a visit from her. By now, Norah would have heard the gossip about Duncan, and her first impulse, Triona thought uneasily, would have been to discuss it with her. It was Melia who told her that Norah had gone with the Fishers to spend some days in the government guest house on the west coast.

'She have a little holiday there,' the cook reported. 'Is nice for she to take a change with friends. Mistress Fisher is a nice nice lady, but she husband make a sad-man face all time.' She giggled, hiding her round black face in her apron. 'People say he 'fraid of the devil if he goes laughing!'

The weather was hot and humid and there was no wind to stir the palm fronds. The two servants became lazy and Triona found herself being unusually sharp with them. Melia sulked and her cooking deteriorated, and the other maid retired to her bed claiming she was suffering from a wild fever which apparently could be cured only by hot milk and rum.

Ram had gone to get married, and Triona realised that she missed the little brown-skinned gardener and his

watchful presence. Not that there was need to be watchful now that Corby had left the island.

No visitors called. The heat was too enervating, and
the 'white folk' stayed in their houses and bungalows,
fanning themselves and thinking of cool English winters.

Triona fought against the fears that beset her since
Flora's visit. Any day now news would come that would
prove Flora had been lying. Until then, there was
nothing to do but try to occupy herself with small
activities. She tried to do some sewing, but her hands
became damp and the needle slipped.

There came one evening when her fears broke
through her restraint. She found it impossible to remain
in the house and decided it would be cooler outside; she
would sleep better after a stroll.

The moon was full, a great silver orb that seemed to
pulsate with dazzling light. Under its luminous splendour the land lay, voluptuous in its beauty. The air was
warm and caressing and scented with the fragrance of
the night-flowering plants, and slowly her burden of
feverish misgiving lightened as she walked along the
path. The cicadas' nightly chorus was muted, as if tuned
to the languorous magic of the night. A faint throbbing of
drums told her some celebration was going on in the
hills. Perhaps it was Ram's wedding feast, she thought.
The night's burnished splendour soothed her mind into a
dreamy state. How beautiful the little island was, and yet
it could be dangerous . . .

Why had she thought of danger? What had suddenly
broken the tranquillity of her mood? She paused
abruptly, feeling a prickling sense of fear.

She started back with a gasp as a man came from the
shadows and she recognised Lew Corby! And Ram was
away!

He came towards her slowly, and she saw the raw lust

in his face and the ugly scar twitch in his cheek and she knew she was in deadly danger. He walked stealthily, like some feline animal stalking its prey. An icy chill invaded her body so that she could not move. As he drew near, she heard him whisper, 'So you would have me arrested if I set foot on your land? You tell the police to hound me out of the island as if I am a mad dog?'

'Go away,' she whispered. 'Don't touch me!'

'But tonight is made for love . . . For a beautiful woman in my arms, a woman of flame—Come with me!'

'*No!*' Her cry died in her throat as he grabbed at her. He dragged her to him, crushing her cruelly against his body. She tried to scream, but fear constricted her throat so that she could make no sound. Silently she fought him. The rank, animal smell of his body sickened her and she became savage, sinking her teeth into his arm. He laughed brutally, and she felt herself being swept off her feet and carried into the tall bamboo plantation. She managed to cry out, but he forced her head against him, smothering her cries. She knew she was near to fainting and, dragging her head back, she called frantically,

'*Duncan!*'

Abruptly she felt the man's arms slacken as if her cry had startled him. Her strength returned, she wrenched herself free and staggered away from him. She heard a hoarse yell and, as her vision cleared, saw her attacker lying on the ground with Duncan standing over him.

For a second she thought her eyes had deceived her, then she cried again, '*Duncan!* Oh Duncan . . . you came!'

'Keep away!' His command made her shrink back as Corby leaped to his feet and lunged at Duncan, and the two men closed in fierce combat. Duncan was the bigger man, but Corby had a snake's lightning strike and sinuous movement, and she screamed as Duncan reeled back from a vicious blow. Corby turned to run but Duncan caught him by his shoulder. Suddenly Triona saw the half-breed's hand go to his belt and the flash of steel. She cried, '*No!*' and, flinging herself forward, she caught the raised arm, deflecting the blow. She was thrown to one side and lay, dazed and with the breath knocked out of her, hearing a thin, high screaming followed by a crash, and then silence broken by Duncan's laboured breathing.

Then he was beside her, raising her gently. 'Triona, are you hurt? My God, I'll kill the brute for this!'

'I am not hurt. Oh Duncan, I called your name . . . But I did not know you were near.' She brushed her disordered hair from her blanched face. 'How . . . When . . . I don't understand . . .'

'Don't try to. I'm going to carry you to the house.' He lifted her and carried her from the shadows into the moon's radiant light.

'Corby,' she whispered. 'He may escape.'

'He will be safe for some time,' he said grimly. 'I'll tie him up and the police can deal with him when they arrive. Lie still, my dearest. You have had a hellish experience, but you are safe now.'

She obeyed, her horror washed away by the over-whelming joy at hearing his voice and feeling his arms around her. He bore her to the house and went to call Melia, whose black face expressed alarm and intense curiosity, and told her to make coffee and bring water to wash the blood from his cheek and raw knuckles.

'It might have been worse,' he said cheerfully, 'if you had not seen that knife. You had no business to do such a rash thing, my girl.'

'He meant to kill you.'

'It takes a lot to kill me. When did he appear?'

'I was walking along the path when I saw him. He

was . . . beastly!' She shuddered, covering her face with her hands as she remembered.

He swore softly, his eyes hard as steel. 'He will pay for this. He'll go to the prison on St Lucia for a long, long time, curse his filthy hide.'

'Corby is a bad bad man,' Melia agreed, coming in with the coffee. 'He a no-good animal. Why you don't kill him, master?'

'He'll probably wish I had,' Duncan said grimly. 'I'll attend to him now. He can spend the night in the stables.'

Triona went to her room to change her torn dress and wash her face and hands. She combed her hair and let it swing about her shoulders in all its shining glory.

Duncan rose slowly as she entered the room, his eyes upon her. His face was discoloured and swollen, and she caught her breath. Then she ran to him, and felt his arms close around her hungrily.

'Duncan, your poor bruised face! Oh, I thought I would never see you again! I have been so afraid!'

He kissed her with a passionate force that set her senses on fire as she clung to him. Fiercely she returned his kisses, pressing her body against him. They were one, their kisses uniting them in passion and longing.

'Why didn't you write to me?' she whispered. 'I waited so long for some word from you.'

He stared, his dark brows drawn in a frown as he said, 'But I did write. A long letter, Triona, telling you everything. How my conviction was quashed after Juan Geira had given evidence, and how I hated having to remain in Port of Spain until the case was closed while I was so longing to be with you.'

Triona's eyes widened. 'You *did* write? I never got your letter, and when the mail from Trinidad came and there was nothing from you, I thought . . . I wondered . . .' She gripped his arm. 'I thought you had decided, perhaps, not to return to Ste-Martine, that you intended to go back to England with Captain Drew!'

'Where in the name of heaven did you get that idea, Triona?'

'It was the wife of the Police Commissioner, at a tea-party at Government House. She said her husband had heard from you about selling Toco, and that you had mentioned you would not be returning . . . That you planned to go back to England.'

Melia entered, carrying a tray with glasses and a bottle, her black face beaming. 'Is good you take a little spirit after such wicked trouble,' she announced firmly. 'Madam had a nasty bad shock, and when a man is fighting he need something to help he get back strength.' She put the tray on the table.

'Thank you, Melia,' Duncan said as he picked up the bottle of rum. 'You had better take a drop of rum yourself after the wicked trouble.'

The cook's smile broadened. 'I done take a small piece of rum already, sir,' she told him, and waddled out chuckling.

'Drink this,' Duncan commanded, handing Triona a glass. When she had drunk a little of the fiery spirit, he sat down beside her, slipping his arm around her as he said, 'Triona, are you certain the Commissioner's wife told you that?'

'Oh yes, dearest, indeed I was. She said her husband had told her.'

'My God, what a fool that woman is! She has the brains of a hen, I have never known her get any of her facts right.' He sprang to his feet and began to pace the room, his eyes hard with anger. 'Her husband is almost as big a fool to tell her anything. I wrote to him about selling Toco, and said I was selling it because I did not mean to continue living in Ste-Martine but would be eventually returning to England.' He faced her. 'I knew you did not wish to remain here, Triona, and neither did I. But surely you did not think—You could not have thought for a moment that I would not return to you?'

She put her hands to her flushed cheeks. 'I—I did not know what to think, Duncan. I was so terribly unhappy when I had no word from you, and then . . .' She dropped her hands and looked up at him, a flash of quick anger in her eyes. 'And then Flora Ellison came and told me she had received a letter from you and you were going back to England with Captain Drew and his wife—and her!'

His face told her the truth before he broke out furiously, 'She said that? She must be mad! I never wrote to her. Why should I? The woman sickens me with her hungry eyes and craving for attention! What made her lie so shamelessly?'

Triona rose swiftly, saying, 'Wait, Duncan, I want to ask Melia something.' She called the cook to the door. 'Melia, was it Mr Ashton who brought my mail some days ago?'

'No, ma'am, Mistress Ellison done bring it. I take it from she myself.'

Triona said, 'Thank you, Melia, you can go.' She turned to face Duncan and, as his eyes met hers, he nodded grimly.

'She took it, my letter from you,' she said slowly. 'She read it—or destroyed it. Oh, how could she! It was wicked, cruel!'

'She is both wicked and cruel.' Duncan's voice was steely. 'I think she must hate you. She is an evil woman, and I refuse to believe Harry Drew offered her a passage on his yacht. Or, if he did, she forced him to.'

'She liked you, and she was jealous of me because she saw you did not return her liking.'

He sat down, pulling her down beside him. 'How could I like her, when I was so deeply in love with the most desirable and lovely woman in the island—in the world?'

She laughed softly as she leaned her bright head against his shoulder. 'Now tell me how you arrived here, and when.'

'Harry Drew brought me,' he said promptly. 'We arrived this evening and I came direct to Forest House, found you missing, and followed you—Thank God I did!'

She raised her head to stare at him. 'Captain Drew brought you? But he was to wait for Flora Ellison in Port of Spain! She has gone to join him and his wife— she left here yesterday—to go back to England with them.'

He shrugged. 'I think Harry's wife changed their plans. Harry was good enough to bring me back as soon as I was free to come. Flora can get a ship from Trinidad and make her own way home.' He grinned. 'One thing is certain. Effie Ashton will not invite her back to Ste-Martine.'

They sat in a silence that was golden with happiness and love. Triona thought of the months of dread and fear with Colin, and the shock and terrible anxiety of Duncan's trial and conviction, and felt the memories slip into oblivion as she rested in Duncan's arms.

At last he sighed and kissed her long and passionately before rising to say, 'I must go to Toco. Mark has lent me a horse. I shall return tomorrow, my dearest, and we shall go into Regina and see Ernest Fisher. You are marrying me as soon as he can arrange it. We have been parted too long. You are mine now and for ever.'

'People will think it strange, Duncan, for me to marry so soon,' she protested.

'To the devil with what people will think! I cannot live without you, Triona. Be ready tomorrow morning.'

When she awoke next morning she wondered for a moment if it had all been a dream, then memory flooded back and she sprang out of bed. She dressed, choosing a cream embroidered Swiss muslin gown and a tiny cream straw hat with lavender ribbons and was waiting for him when he drove up to the house.

That morning she had given her widow's weeds to the servants. Never again would she wear black. She had mourned sincerely for the Colin of their early marriage; now her mourning was over and her future lay with the man for whom she felt a depth of passionate love such as she had never before known. She and Colin had been boy and girl lovers; now she was a woman, with a woman's primitive longing for the love of the man who filled her heart.

Duncan's eyes told her she was beautiful. She sat beside him as they drove into the town, her heart too full for words.

The vicar appeared startled and somewhat disapproving. 'It is most unusual. The period of mourning . . .'

His wife broke in to say, 'Oh, do not be so stuffy, Ernest dear. We all know how much Mrs Brooks has had to suffer in the past.'

Her husband looked at her in scandalised surprise. 'My dear, it is not quite—er—proper to say such a thing.'

'Well, I've just said it. Both Mrs Brooks and Mr Ross have been through great troubles and they love each other and want to marry. I think you should do it as soon as you can.'

Her husband protested, but feebly, and the day for the ceremony was settled.

Mrs Fisher embraced Triona before she left, and whispered, 'My dear, I am so glad for you. Ernest feels he *must* disapprove as part of his duty, but it need not worry you.'

As they left the Fishers' house, Triona said happily, 'Now we must call upon Norah. Unless we should call at the police station first.'

'Don't worry about that,' he told her grimly. 'They have already attended to Corby who, I am glad to say, was in a very poor condition.'

Norah flew to embrace Triona, crying, 'So he's come back to you at last! For mercy's sake, Duncan, what have you done to your face?'

He began to explain the events of the night, while Norah's eyes grew rounder and her plump cheeks redder. When he had done, she rang the bell for the servant.

'We'll have luncheon at once,' she stated firmly. 'Excitement always gives me a fearful appetite. Dear God, what a terrible experience for you, Triona! If Duncan hadn't come when he did . . . Ah, but we won't dwell on that. And so you are to marry at once, and rightly so, for aren't you made for each other. Tell me, do you plan to leave the West Indies at once?'

'Not at once, but soon,' Duncan said. 'I have a brother in Bristol who is in the importing business, and he has often suggested that I join him. He thinks my knowledge of these islands and their products will be useful.'

'But won't you have to sell Toco and Forest Estates first?'

'Yes, and that is where lady luck has taken a hand.' He turned to Triona. 'There was a letter waiting for me from my lawyer. The government plan for an experimental agricultural estate has gone through, and an offer has been made for both Toco and Forest Estates. It is an excellent offer, and we shall accept it.'

'Just listen to him!' Norah exclaimed. 'Isn't he talking like a husband already.'

They were having coffee when Mark and Effie Ashton were shown into the room. Effie danced up to Duncan, her pretty face alight, as she cried,

'So you *did* come back! Of course I knew you would, and it was all silly jealousy on Flora's part. Did you know, Triona, that she told us she had received a letter from Duncan?'

'I think she did,' Triona told her, 'only it was meant for me.' She revealed her suspicions of Flora having withheld the letter.

'She *must* have taken it,' Effie said, shocked. 'Mark was going to take the mail up to Forest House, but she insisted on delivering it. How *wicked* of her! And all her lies about Duncan. The odd thing was that I *did* hear a rumour from someone—I believe it was the Commissioner's wife—that Duncan did not mean to return, and I was *so* upset. And then Mark met the Commissioner, who said his wife *always* got things wrong because she never listened properly.'

'That little ninny would get her own name wrong,' Norah remarked caustically. 'But tell me, now, did Mrs Ellison know Captain Drew intended to come back here, bringing Duncan, before she dashed off to Port of Spain?'

'No, she didn't,' Effie said. 'She quite *bullied* poor Harry about offering her a passage in his yacht. She said she would meet him in Port of Spain and he was to show her around the island first. But when Harry told his wife, she would have none of it. She doesn't like Flora.'

Norah was chuckling. 'So the lovely Mrs Flora Ellison will have to view the island alone.'

'Knowing Flora,' commented Mark, 'I doubt if she will view it alone. I'm afraid she has behaved very badly indeed, and she might have made trouble between Harry and his wife if she had gone with them. I hold no brief for my sister. She has always been the stormy petrel of our family.'

'Ah well, she's one who will always fall on her feet,' Norah said. 'She'll make no more trouble here. So there is to be a wedding and a honeymoon voyage back to England. Isn't that a happy ending for Triona and Duncan?'

'It is indeed,' Effie agreed, smiling at Triona. 'We shall all miss you dreadfully.'

Norah nodded. 'But there won't be one who won't wish you happiness, my dears.'

The wedding was a very quiet one, with only Norah, Mrs Fisher and the Ashtons present. Three weeks later Triona found herself aboard Captain Jones's shabby little boat en route for St Lucia, where they would join the Cunard liner. Duncan had been impatient to leave Ste-Martine, and had put the business of the two estates in the lawyer's hands.

Triona stood at the ship's rail watching the island drift past, its colours jewel-bright in the morning sunlight. Slowly the jade sea widened the gap between the ship and the white, palm-fringed shore as they left Carib Bay and rounded the point to turn north. The long ranges of island forest had the dazzling shimmer of a peacock's tail as the little ship followed the coastline, and she could see the flame trees threading through the green jungle like small fires. They passed Forest, then Toco, and the coral reef where the sun sent rainbows through the spume.

Impulsively she turned to Duncan, and asked, 'Are you sad to leave the island, my dearest?'

He shook his head, his arm tightening around her. 'No. All my happiness is here.' He bent to kiss her. 'Do *you* have any regrets?'

'No, none. Did you know Norah is planning to come over next year? She says she might even consider settling in Ireland, and could pay us a visit.'

'I hope she will. Tell me, my Lady of Flame, will you be content to see me become a conventional, prudent business man?'

She laughed softly. 'My darling, you will never be conventional; and prudence is not one of your virtues, I fear.'

'Tell me when I have been imprudent,' he demanded.

She flashed him a teasing smile as she said, 'The day you fell in love with a woman whose hair was the colour of the Flame of the Forest.'

'The woman who disliked and mistrusted me,' he reminded her.

'A woman who had never known what true love was until she met you, who had never loved with her whole heart before.'

'Is that true?' His voice was urgent. 'Sometimes I cannot believe it, Triona. Is it true?'

She turned and slipped her arms around his neck, drawing his face down to hers as she said softly, 'It is true, my most beloved husband, now and for ever.'

Mills & Boon

Your chance to step into the past Take 2 Books FREE

Discover a world long vanished. An age of chivalry and intrigue, powerful desires and exotic locations. Read about true love found by soldiers and statesmen, princesses and serving girls. All written as only Mills & Boon's top-selling authors know how. Become a regular reader of Mills & Boon Masquerade Historical Romances and enjoy 4 superb, new titles every two months, plus a whole range of special benefits: your very own personal membership card entitles you to a regular free newsletter packed with recipes, competitions, exclusive book offers plus other bargain offers and big cash savings.

AND an Introductory FREE GIFT for YOU.
Turn over the page for details.